I0623094

STOLEN PALLOR

SEAN EADS AND JOSHUA VIOLA

Copyright © 2024 by Sean Eads and Joshua Viola

First Edition

All rights reserved

ISBN: 978-1-940250-64-9

This book is a work of fiction. Names, characters, business organizations, places, events and incidents either are the product of the author's imagination or are used fictitiously. Any resemblance to actual persons, living or dead, events or locales is entirely coincidental.

Cover Art by Mushfiq A.K.

Interior Layout by Lori Michelle
www.TheAuthorsAlley.com

Printed in the United States of America

Visit us on the web at:
www.bloodboundbooks.net
https://www.bloodgutsandstory.com/

From Sean: For Kyle Hembree.

From Joshua: For my husband, Aaron.

"**JESUS CHRIST**, *look at the crowd. With these glass walls, I feel like a fish in an overstuffed aquarium. There must be 300 people in here. What's the limit?"*

"No one's counting at a thing like this," Dad says, unseen. "Do I look like the fire marshal? Where is Ben, anyway? How the hell did he get out of this? He call in sick too?"

The most dignified of all dignitaries wear black tuxedos with red roses pinned to their lapels. Twenty-nine of them gather near the painting, draped in a black curtain. The mystery canvas, five feet long and six feet wide, commands a healthy portion of the thirty-foot dais. The Who's Who schmooze near it. All those bright roses. Dad's voice again comes from nowhere. "Looks like I can't loiter down here any longer. Time to join the bouquet. Someone keep an eye on Cole, he wants to be here even less than me."

Then a glimpse of Dad, moving up on the dais, taking a position next to the mayor. The two men exchange words and point at the glass walls and ceiling. The whole building also covered by black cloth. Starless, moonless night. Almost can't believe there's sunlight beyond the fabric. A neat thing really, like being under a pitch-black circus tent. Neat things must be conceded. Light comes from somewhere. No obvious lightbulbs or lamps. How is the room lit?

1

STOLEN PALLOR

Two hundred people but somehow a thousand smiles. Some directed at the room's only child. People smile too damn much. They smile when they're happy. They smile when they're sad. For some reason they smile when they're angry. They smile when they're feeling embarrassed or humiliated or awkward. They smile most when they sense the presence of someone who doesn't feel like smiling. The frown on a petulant thirteen-year-old boy's face is gasoline for smiling strangers. Assuming they deign to notice such pests.

Dad's still up there beside the mayor, stiff and unnatural like some portrait artist's abducted model. A big bear squeezed into a navy-blue uniform, the badge of his authority gleaming with bright silver polish above his right breast. There's a door to the far left that says Bathroom. *No recollection of that. Another new detail, delivered as promised. The room is full of them. The odor of an old woman passing by in a red dress to his right. A man's annoying persistent cough. The sense of a shadow lurking above, concealed by the black backdrop. Anticipation builds inside the glass walls. Excited cocktail hour chatter, like the voices of the dead speaking across a gulf of centuries—*

"Have you heard of the artist? They say—"

"From Europe, yes. Belgium, maybe?"

"I think it's very probable he is in the room now. What artist could resist? Enigmatic as he's supposed to be, you'd never—"

"Totally dedicated to anonymity. It is the work and work alone that—"

Then there's a memory within a memory, the recollection of an argument from two hours earlier.

"Why do I have to be there?"

"Because if I suffer, you suffer. It's in the contract, Cole."

"What about Mom's death? Was that in the contract, too?"

"Third clause on page eight, right column. Now get dressed. This morning's a big deal."

What a nasty thing to say to Dad, and a stale card to play. It worked most times when he was seven, eight and nine. No trump card lasts forever. Is being here all that obnoxious? Isn't history being made? New Florence outbid every city and museum on Earth to host this event. The Directorate triumphed over the Louvre. Art is the great sea that raises all ships. The mayor is proclaiming that through the microphone right now. The attendees applaud. Dad offers a polite clap; the rose-garnished dignitaries show more enthusiasm. For this is their combined achievement. A sudden sense of astromechanics at play. Art's mighty rocket has launched. The second stage boosters just fired. Separation nears.

The curtains will drop.

Thousands of people wait on the other side of the glass, clamoring for a glimpse of the promised masterpiece. But the insiders will have it first. Here and there designated cameramen with pre-approved lenses move through the audience, photographing the creme-de-la-creme sipping champagne from fluted crystal.

"And we really don't know what he looks like, or if he is a he?"

"Not the slightest clue."

"Amazing. Astounding."

The artist might be on another continent. Then again, he or she might be here. The possibility makes sly glances abundant. Like something out of a locked room murder mystery. Is he among us? Wouldn't it be something if at least one person sized him up as a candidate? Yes, the great artist New Florence built a glass house for and then draped in black cloth is a child prodigy. Behold him now!

He sees himself jumping onto the dais to rip the cloth away just to see what the crowd will buy. Rich people buy everything.

"It seems, at long last, the moment has arrived. We best be synchronized."

His father, the mayor, and the dignitaries now

orchestrate themselves around the painting. Several hands pinch the cloth and wait. The crowd moves forward, a silent wave that leaves him alone near the back of the room. He retreats further until his back touches the glass. Maybe the thing to do is be the one person looking out at the crowd when the curtain drops. Waving. Making a face. Giving the finger. Anything to draw the eye first and steal a little thunder.

There must be a hundred faces waiting to see through the very pane he stands before. Will both curtains really fall at the same time? That's the promise. A double revealing.

"Get ready for a new morning for New Florence, my friends. I'm now allowed to tell you the name of the piece. Revel in having this knowledge before the rest of the world. The painting is called Gone By Morning. But I think for those of us privileged to share this special moment, the memories of this morning will never leave."

The sense of a moving shadow again. Above them. Not inside the room, not quite outside of it. Somewhere. Everywhere. A terrible thing. An absolute wrongness. As the mayor cries, "Now!" Dad and the others pull. The cloth slips away from the ceiling as well. Impressive timing that reveals the painting and gallery interior all at once as sudden sunlight bathes them.

Followed by so many screams.

There's an image within the mounted frame, but already lost to a conquering fire. More smoke than possible comes from the canvas, oily vapors as thick and heavy as genie mist rising from some mishandled lamp. "The doors won't open! Why won't the goddamn doors open?" Dad's almost alone on the dais, choking, his left forearm across his face as his right hand beats his dress coat against the fire. The mayor is burning and so are the dignitaries, their roses charring. So much deafening screaming and yet, even now, a new detail: the delicate and discreet crunches made by fluted crystal when crushed under fearful heels.

The flames have dominion across the room now, creeping up legs, devouring black dress pants, nibbling the hems of evening gowns worn on a fateful morning. Where's Dad? Smoke is conquering their airtight world. Through it many dark shapes wander, horrific pantomimes. Hands slap and pound the glass from without. Someone takes a heavy rock and pitches it at the pane without making a scratch. Someone fires a gun once. The glass stands defiant. Fires a second time. As effective as shooting up a sand dune, and what is glass after all? All windows are hourglasses whose time is frozen. As in a dream.

He's gifted one final new detail, a resurrected memory of what he was thinking before losing consciousness. A year earlier, he'd seen glass coffins on some website and thought it funny. He'd shown Dad and the two of them had a good laugh. Mom was gone long enough now that it was okay to joke about death sometimes. So glass coffins. What a way to get buried.

He looks up at the glass ceiling.
Buried.
The smoke.
The fire.
Eternity inside glass.
No, it isn't funny.
Dad, I love you.

Fuck bedrooms with east-facing windows and the dipshits who don't buy blinds for them, Cole Sharpe thought, as the light struck his face and roused him from a sleepy, drunken stupor. He pressed his right forearm over his eyes and extended a middle finger before flopping over, expecting the heat of Mikey's body. His hand swept over cold sheets. Frowning, keeping his eyes shut, Cole listened for sounds beyond the bedroom door. The shower wasn't going. The TV wasn't on. No olfactory evidence the coffee maker was in recent use.

In short, Mr. Detective: your trick is gone.

And if past behavior prognosticated anything, so was some cash from Cole's wallet.

Mikey absconding without saying goodbye wasn't unique, since he often worked a 4AM bakery shift, a job he'd taken at Cole's own insistence that he try to walk the straight and narrow. But this morning he was supposed to stay and help Cole resolve the dream. That had been the whole point of their get-together.

"Thanks for nothing," he said, rolling onto his back, angling his face out of the sunlight as he sought answers in the ceiling's textured drywall.

Okay, he thought. Not *nothing*. Drinks had been fun, and Mikey's blowjob skills were transcendent. He always joked he specialized in all iterations of *head*.

"It's this goddamn dream, man," Cole told him when they met at a bar down the street.

"The gallery fire nightmare?"

"I'll go months without having it, then something triggers it every night for weeks. I think frustrations with my new case is bringing it up this time and I can't sleep or concentrate. Twenty years of this bullshit. I'm just ready to be done."

"It's sabotaged your life."

"The fire sabotaged my life. The dream just keeps reminding me."

Mikey nodded. He was in his late 20s, a few years younger than Cole, with expressive brown eyes and a good heart capable of justifying minor acts of criminality. As he often said, "There's not much bread in making bread."

"So, you want me to take care of your problem?"

Cole had stiffened. Yes, of course that's what he wanted.

Right?

Mikey put his hand to his forehead, closed his eyes and said, "I sense . . . wavering."

"Don't need psychic powers for that. But—*can you?*"

"I haven't messed with dreams very much. I have some ideas, though. Let's go back to your place. Have some fun. I'll explain how I think this might go down and you can decide if treatment's right for you."

"You make it sound like an E.D. clinic pitch."

"If the dream was causing you *that* problem, I'd have a personal vendetta against it."

Cole finished his beer. "Glad to know you're helping me out of your own self-interest."

Mikey answered with a rueful laugh. "Self-interest is like a shapeshifter. It takes many forms. You're a terrible burden to me, Cole. First, you know my secret. Second, I'm into you, but you won't give me the time of day unless you need something."

"That's not true!"

"'Mikey, I want to go into Midnight Village again for a look around. Will you drop whatever it is you're doing to be my passport?' 'Mikey, I'm feeling a little horny, want to help me out?' 'Mikey, I've got this terrible dream, can you get rid of it for me?'"

Cole laughed at the exaggerated impression. Mikey winked at him.

"You could find a much better use for a guy with my abilities in your line of work," Mikey continued. "I can walk the straight and narrow. The narrow, anyway."

"Maybe one day."

After the sex was over and Mikey's psychic procedure's details established, they lay in bed facing each other in silence. A minute passed. Mikey moved to touch Cole's head, an action that caused Cole to flinch.

"Relax," Mikey said. "I wouldn't do it without your permission."

He stroked Cole's hair in silence. A drowsiness stole over Cole. Before he knew it, he fell asleep. The dream was ready like some pouncing assassin hiding behind a door, jolting him awake. He found Mikey still in place, still silent, still stroking his hair.

"Please get rid of it for me," Cole said.

"Just think of the dream. All the details as best you remember them. And close your eyes. Now start talking."

"There are a lot of people. I don't see their faces. Just old people."

"This time you will. Each and every face as clear as a photo. The dream's going to be very real. Colors, smells, sounds. It will be awful but I'm going to dredge what's inside in order to purge it. Like sucking venom out of a snake bite."

Keeping his eyes shut, Cole felt ten points of sudden heat across his skull as Mikey placed both hands on his head. His fingertips felt like lit cigarettes being stubbed out against Cole's skin. He gritted his teeth. Fascination kept him pushing through the pain.

"The dream may last all night. It doesn't matter what the original time span was. Even five minutes will go on for hours. When you wake up, you'll tell me everything you remember. When you're finished, the dream will be gone forever."

And in fact, as Cole got out of bed now, the urge to describe the dream was so real and insistent that he started talking to himself. A buzzing sensation tingled the roof of his mouth. "The woman next to me, she was in a green dress, and she had a string of pearls the same color as her hair. She was holding this little fluted crystal glass and—Mikey? Mikey?"

He opened the bedroom door, stepped into the hallway and said, "Mikey?" He checked the bathroom, kitchen and living room.

Mikey didn't even leave a note.

"The room was lit, but I don't know how. Not a light bulb in the place, and when I looked up all I could see was the heavy blackness of the drape pressing down. I remember—damnit, Mikey—"

8

Cole slumped against a wall. Echoes of the dying sounded in his ears. Flashes of fire strobed across his vision. He smelled cooking flesh and his stomach churned. Against these horrors, however, rose the sound of his father's voice and laugh, more perfect than any digital recording. Little details of his father's face, like the mole near his right temple, invisible except right after haircuts. The wafting odor of his father's aftershave. These memories were new and wonderful discoveries no matter the context. Did he want to give them up forever? Couldn't Mikey maybe save these elements and delete the rest?

"Time for me to join the bouquet," Cole said, starting to chuckle. But he swore he heard his father's voice coming from his mouth, and it shocked him into clapping a hand over his lips.

Time for me to join the bouquet.

This time Dad's voice sounded from behind him with such clarity that he turned, expecting him in the hallway. Dad was there, engulfed in flames. Cole shouted as the figure collapsed in a fiery heap like some wood statue. The carpet was burning. His eardrums ached from a sudden explosion, the mad frenzy of hands beating on the glass walls from without and within.

The apartment was lost in smoke and fire. Pantomime figures and shadow puppets reached for him, their silhouette arms seeking safety through the flames. Cole fell and kicked, about to scream. He felt like he was in a Bible story, something his mom read to him as a kid all the time. His belief in any of that stuff ended when she did.

"Not real, not real," Cole said, clenching his jaw.

He slapped himself across the face and the blow brought him back to his mundane apartment with its beige, soiled carpet. He took a few breaths to slow his pulse.

He moved into the kitchen, taking a tightrope walker's careful linear tread. He turned on his Keurig. In the sound of its activation, he heard the crowd's murmurs of anticipation. When he closed the pod lid, he saw the curtain drop. Fire streamed into the mug and clouds of smoke rose around him. He was a boy again, trapped in glass, pounding on the windows and calling for his father.

"Not real, goddamnit!"

The hallucination ended.

His phone chimed in the bedroom.

Mikey, he thought, hurrying down the hall. Cole discovered a disappointing reality when he saw the caller ID.

Amistead Dimwitter.

The chairman of the Directorate.

He put the phone to his ear but as he answered he felt like he was blowing inhaled smoke from his lungs and broke into a coughing fit.

"Mr. Sharpe? Mr. Sharpe, are you okay?"

Cole pounded on his chest. "Sorry, just a bad connection here. It's better now."

"Mr. Sharpe, can you meet me at the West Gallery right away?"

Cole shifted the phone to his other ear, about to say no. Finding Mikey had to be his priority.

"I'm a bit occupied at the moment. What's—"

"This is urgent, Mr. Sharpe. It's happening again. It's happening *now*."

"I'm on my way."

Every city claims a love affair with art. Of course, they have their museums and art galleries, public and private, touristy and hip, catering to all tastes. If the affair deepens to romance, one begins to find trendy downtown neighborhood *scenes:* multicultural murals revitalizing decaying brick walls, embossed sound barriers along certain stretches of highway.

Founded 175 years ago, New Florence had an immediate, shotgun marriage to art whose matrimonial bonds continued to strengthen. The walk to the West Gallery was less than a mile, and Cole went down sidewalks still covered in bright chalk drawings of animals and faces, shapes and figures, the result of the Directorate's continuous *Your Street, Your Imagination* childhood expression campaign. Year round across the city, one could not avoid stepping on colorful depictions of roses and sunshine, smiles, summer days. Even the homeless and indigent were issued boxes of chalk along with bottled water and a meal and encouraged to sketch out dreams of brighter days in whatever discreet corner they'd spend their nights. *Art belongs to the people. Art feeds the public heart.* One of the Directorate's many slogans. Oftentimes, Cole wanted to ask if chalk was edible when the public stomach rumbled late on a chilly, unsheltered night.

As he trespassed across all this happiness, Cole's mood favored washing every concrete square clean. He pulled the collar of his wool coat tight. Tidings of winter were no longer reserved to late night temperature dips. The morning's brightness was sharpened and clarified by the air's chill, and gray frost limned the windshields of curbside cars. Seeing traces of his breath before him, all the warm depictions at his feet seemed like too much desperate pining for a vanquished season.

Art did not lord itself over mere sidewalks in New Florence. Decades of architectural intent and planning had turned the city skyline into layered rows of forty multi-colored skyscrapers internationally renowned as *The Crayon Box*. The hydrophobic film coatings on the windows were tinted to reflect and refract the sunlight's propagation, so that each expansive pane framed a nebula reminiscent of oil stains on asphalt. Below, on the no less exalted ground, painters set up easels in the financial district. Sketch artists populated the parks, caricaturists the public areas outside the basketball arena and football stadium, and hopeful opportunists made customized watercolor postcards across the city's tourist destinations.

No utility box or pole went undecorated, the light rail trains and buses were rainbow streaks in their transit, and the city dumps were picked clean by scavengers dedicated to upcycling and mixed-media collages.

Yes, New Florence had married art, and its children included more than 300 galleries and museums. Even the city council was a step down in power from the Gallery Directorate, that august assembly of directors of the thirty largest galleries, whose combined collections boasted thousands of paintings assessed at over a billion dollars. The Directorate had outbid the Louvre for rare finds, but their true pride was in discovering and curating unknown painters and turning them into superstars through the sheer power of their interest. They had proved their ability to do this several times without a misstep until—

Cole found last night's dream trying to assert itself over his vision. He forced himself to keep walking even as the sidewalk turned to fire under his feet. Smoke invaded his nostrils again, dizzying him until he had to stop and lean against an adjacent car. He reached his hand into his coat pocket and gripped a piece of cold metal he always kept with him. It fit into the palm of his hand and weighed almost nothing, but Cole always thought of it as his anchor. Three firm squeezes vanquished the hallucinations and he marched forward.

The West Gallery came into view. He could hear Dimwitter's voice in his head from two weeks ago, explaining how it was the Directorate's oldest building and still housed its original collection. Cole had been amused, not by the details but the practiced way Dimwitter gave them, as if Cole were there for a tour rather than investigating what Dimwitter called a *peculiarity*.

"The North, South and East Galleries have five times West's capacity, and even they're dwarfed by Central. It has almost 900,000 square feet of exhibit space, did you know that?"

"I did not."

"It's true. I oversaw the expansion myself. I—"
"You called me because of a problem."
"Oh yes, that."

Sudden nervousness in his voice and demeanor. Cole had a genuine curiosity about what constituted a *problem* for rarified men like Dimwitter. Why was he calling a private investigator with fifty online reviews and a 3.6 star rating? Not that these questions mattered too much after he accepted Cole's consultation fee up front.

The West Gallery had ashen gray carpet in the lobby and eggshell white walls. The individual gallery floors were a continuous gray and yellow checkerboard pattern of vinyl tiles. The building's one pretension was the ornate gilt crown molding that ran from room to room in seamless transition like connective tissue. Cole felt Dimwitter fighting the urge to give him a whole spiel about the decor. Instead, they went down a nondescript hallway to a security room. The guard there already had a video waiting.

A woman was standing in front of a painting. Cole shifted in his seat, expecting something to happen.

She went on standing.

Five minutes passed.

"This goes on for a few hours," Dimwitter said.

"How do you tolerate the nonstop action around here?"

Dimwitter told the guard to fast-forward through the footage. The woman stood unswaying and statue-still while people came and went at exaggerated speed. Some seemed to stop and regard her before leaving.

"The staff took an embarrassing amount of time realizing she'd not moved in hours. Perhaps I shouldn't be so harsh. People often stop in front of paintings and stare, trying to understand what they're seeing, trying to lose themselves in interpretation."

"Trying not to feel stupid," Cole said.

Dimwitter grunted. Cole expected some reproach, a recitation of one of the Directorate's many mottos, like *Art can only serve to enlighten.*

"Twelve attendants staffed the floor that morning. They switch rooms every ten minutes, so it was a few rotations before anyone realized her . . . predicament. You can see they try addressing her."

Cole nodded, watching. The accelerated footage now showed the arrival of police and paramedics.

"Let it play in real time from here," Dimwitter said. "Watch what happens. She doesn't respond to any stimulus until the EMTS maneuver her onto the gurney. Then she starts thrashing."

Cole leaned toward the monitor. "When she's forced to lose eye contact with the painting."

The woman bucked against the restraints until she was wheeled away. The space of her absence felt enormous on the screen.

"Where is she now?"

"We don't know. We followed up with the hospital, but it seems she snuck away without being discharged. Not seen since."

"The date on the recording is from two weeks ago. Bit of a late start if you want me to find her."

"While the Directorate cares about every citizen of New Florence, one patron's strange antics wouldn't compel us to consult a detective. I've called you, Mr. Sharpe, because we've since seen three more occurrences of the same behavior."

Cole sat back. "Same room? Same painting?"

"No. But all in the West Gallery. It's most disconcerting."

Dimwitter had the videos placed on a flash drive, and Cole watched them over and over at home, gritting his teeth at poor angles that caught profiles and backs but never showed the painting itself. The next day he returned to have Dimwitter show him the suspect pieces—an Impressionistic view of a field, an austere portrait of peasant life (in the mode of Rembrandt, Dimwitter was quick to explain), and an architectural sketch of a cathedral.

"Are you aware of any connection between these paintings?"

"In what way, Mr. Sharpe? They come from very different eras and countries."

"Were they purchased from a private collection?"

"The piece by Auguste Bendrozol is among the Directorate's earliest purchases. It came to the gallery 120 years ago. The other two are far newer in comparison. The landscape work is so captivating I can understand anyone wanting to stare at it for hours, getting lost in the expert brushstrokes . . . "

Cole tuned Dimwitter out as he went back and forth taking photos, videos, and measurements of the paintings. Meanwhile, Dimwitter's staff had fulfilled Cole's request to cross-reference the video timestamps with the gallery's receipts to come up with possible names for the three individuals: Philip Schaefer, Amanda Barden, and Carl Quirk. These shots in the dark proved accurate. Cole discovered all three were reported missing by their families.

Art galleries, it seemed, were becoming more dangerous all the time.

Cole's focus had been on uncovering possible connections between the four people, but he'd found nothing since a follow-up meeting with Dimwitter last week. The dream had plagued his sleep from the first day of the investigation, destroying his concentration. Maybe this new victim would provide a breakthrough to solve the case. Regardless of Mikey's solution, the dream might go away on its own if he could put this mystery behind him.

An incentive almost as good as cash.

Dimwitter met Cole in the lobby and led him into the Founders' Room. It was sealed off with three traffic cones, four stanchions, and a sign that said *Temporarily*

Unavailable. Dimwitter maneuvered around the obstructions, again in tourist guide mode. "This gallery of self-portraits is dedicated to the fifteen men who signed New Florence's charter. On your right, you'll see Payne Alhuile."

"And then Alex Pentura and Thomas DiLeppo," Cole said, annoyed at Dimwitter's evident surprise. "It's not esoteric knowledge. I grew up in New Florence. I took all the usual school field trips to the galleries, including West."

Those field trips used to make him shake and often he'd duck into the restroom to vomit. The fifteen founders had seemed like a group of murderers to him and only Pentura and DiLeppo remained in his memory. The rest were lost in the fog of useless schoolboy knowledge, information discarded after the tests were over.

But he did recognize the painting of Royland Gerald Bivvens.

His self-portrait dominated the room, several times the size of the rest. Not so much hung on the wall as wedged between the floor and the ceiling, the canvas guarded by a heavy gilt frame of gold leaf and beveled ridges, overdone and busy like Victorian wallpaper. As they approached the painting and the woman standing there, Dimwitter lapsed into old habits. "Baroque style frame, meant to accentuate a sensuous grandeur, though the painting itself seems to imitate the mannerisms of—"

"I'm really not interested now," Cole said, raising a hand in surrender. "Unless it's important to the case."

Dimwitter squared his shoulders and drew back like some offended butler. "Mr. Bivvens is very important to the history of New Florence. All the founders were artists, of course, but his talent was superior. This piece reflects the intensity of his determination. Many have stood and admired it."

Cole looked at the catatonic woman. "She seems like a big fan. How are you doing, ma'am? That's some frame, isn't it?"

"We didn't want to summon an ambulance until you

could see for yourself. That's the right decision, isn't it? No real reason to call medical help for someone just standing here."

"Sound reasoning," Cole said, giving the director a little clap on the shoulder. "What's her name?"

"We don't know yet."

"When did she get here?"

"Right when we opened."

"First in line?"

"No."

"Did she come straight to this painting?"

"The gallery attendants remember her looking around three other rooms, but at a much faster pace than is typical."

"I'd like to see the recording, but I don't want to be away from her for very long."

"I can have the footage sent to your phone."

Dimwitter left and Cole turned his full attention to the woman. She looked to be in her mid-thirties, with straight brown hair cut shoulder-length. Smart attire, a dark blue pants suit with a simple gold brooch pinned on the lapel. The brooch had a red gem insert, ruby or garnet or ornamental glass. Cole raised his phone to photograph it.

As he finished, the security camera file arrived. Cole stepped away a few feet to study the ten-minute recording. Around the halfway mark he had the vague sense of Dimwitter standing next to him. As the footage concluded, the director cleared his throat and said, "Is it helpful?"

"Seems like she's searching, right? No real interest in the paintings. Her body language reminds me of someone trying to spot a face in a crowd."

"You think she came for a rendezvous?"

"See how she stops and looks back and forth when she enters the new gallery? The pause, the way she cocks her head? Then turning in a new direction. There's more at work here. She's acting like she's following a sound. Maybe a voice from the painting."

"Excuse me?"

Cole activated the flashlight on his phone and held it up to the woman's eyes, moving them back and forth. Dimwitter leaned forward just a little, peering.

"Notice the eyes?"

"They look glossy and distant."

"She's blinking. There's also just the *slightest* movement from right to left, which suggests language processing."

"Doesn't that just mean she's hearing us?"

"Then quit talking and keep watching."

They stood there in silent observation. The eyes continued their minute shifting.

"I don't see what that proves," Dimwitter said. "Even when the gallery is quiet, subtle sounds abound. Air flow and—"

"This woman is hearing something besides the HVAC system. I'm sure of it. Maybe it was something she heard the moment she walked into the building—or perhaps even from home. My guess is it was at some point in-between. She's dressed like a professional, something along the lines of a corporate executive or a lawyer. I don't think she was intending to visit the gallery when she picked out her outfit. Whatever drew her here exerted its influence a bit later. Maybe in the car."

"Assuming she has a car."

"You're right," Cole said. "Let's quit making assumptions and find out a little more about her."

The lady's purse remained slung over her right shoulder. Cole went to open it and Dimwitter flinched.

"That's inappropriate."

"It's not like I'm robbing her," Cole said.

Dimwitter radiated tangible waves of nervousness as Cole checked her purse and pulled out a driver's license. "Susan Wills," he said, making a note of her address. Dimwitter pulled the purse away.

"You *can't* do this," he said. "I'm sure it's illegal."

Cole just stopped himself from rolling his eyes. "The law says silence gives consent, right?"

"I don't know."

"I can tell you that it does. And so, Ms. Wills, is it okay if I look through your purse to learn a little more about you?"

The lady went on staring at the painting and Royland G. Bivvens maintained the glare of a disapproving patriarch.

"Sounds like a yes to me. Scrounging through a woman's purse won't be the worst thing I do before this is over. Who knows who I'll have to fuck or kill to solve the case."

Dimwitter's sudden pallor was just what Cole wanted to see, and it almost made him laugh. The director knew about the world through art, frolicking all day among pastoral scenes and pointless abstractions and portraits of people long turned to dust. Such men were easy to bluff.

Dimwitter surrendered the purse.

"This could be a dangerous game we're playing," Cole said, mustering solemnity into his tone. "We can't assume anything. Sometimes possibilities have to rule themselves out before—"

"You have your father's sureness."

Cole stopped rifling through the contents, but his stare seemed to discover a deeper interior as he comprehended Dimwitter's meaning.

"We were younger men then," the director said, moving to Cole's right. A smug nostalgia entered his tone, like he was deigning Cole with a glimpse of a shared past. "I met him when I was the Director of the Donovan Gallery. Back then it was so small I almost didn't qualify as a member of the Directorate. He came to investigate an act of vandalism. Someone broke into Donovan and ruined several paintings. A shocking crime."

"But Dad solved it."

"No. I'm afraid his time was shorter than he knew. Less than a month later—"

Cole found a sudden reek of acrid smoke in his nose. Shadows writhed at the fringe of his vision. He shoved his right hand into his coat pocket and gripped the metal. The hallucinations receded. Dimwitter was still talking, a tour guide of the past now, explaining how every member of the Directorate died that day.

Except himself.

"I was sick with a very bad cold. I remember cursing my illness at 6AM, then thanking it for saving my life by noon. The Directorate worked so hard to secure the *Gone By Morning* exhibit to New Florence. It should have been one of our crowning achievements in New Florence's eternal cultural climb. Instead, it became the single greatest tragedy in the art world since the Momart Fire. Of course, no one died in Momart—"

"Art got them killed."

"Mr. Sharpe!" Cole stared him down until the director found something to look at on the floor.

Cole had to check his roiling anger. He wanted to knock any memory of his dad out of Dimwitter's head. He wished he could make Dimwitter experience the dream in full, show him just what he'd missed because of the sniffles.

"I better take it alone from here," he said.

Without raising his head, Dimwitter asked what the next steps were.

"It's a waiting game now. I intend to sit here and observe Ms. Wills until she moves again, and then I'm going to follow her. Maybe she'll lead me to the others."

"That's it?"

"What else did you expect?"

"I don't know. I thought perhaps detectives had more tools at their disposal."

"Detectives have databases, persistence, imagination, and observation skills. What do you want me to do, produce a magical amulet out of my pocket that breaks the spell she's under?"

"How long will you stay?"

"As long as necessary."

Dimwitter looked at the looming self-portrait. "What if she doesn't move all night? I can't go on keeping the Founders' Room closed to the public."

Cole grinned. "Reopen it as a piece of performance art. Call it *Captured Audience*. Art's all about marketing gimmicks, right? Like a glass building covered in a drape to house a painting by some no-name artist."

This earned an icy glare from Dimwitter.

"Yes. You're *very* much like your father."

I don't have to like him, but it won't help the case if we're at war with each other, Cole thought. He offered a smile and pointed at the painting.

"He was the youngest founder, wasn't he?"

"Yes."

"The one who went mad."

Dimwitter's shoulders sagged a little. Cole chose to interpret it as his coldness thawing. "He died on his 60th birthday after weeks ingesting great quantities of paint."

"Sounds like madness to me."

"When he was asked why he was doing it, he's supposed to have licked his palette, smearing a rainbow across his tongue. Then, his legendary answer: 'How else can I paint my soul?' Is that madness, Mr. Sharpe—or the genius that set a pathetic, struggling artist's colony on the path to its present greatness?"

Dimwitter's lower lip trembled. He seemed on the verge of tears and excused himself. Once Cole was alone with the woman, he was struck by the room's stillness. It had a depth, a thickness. He snapped his fingers twice and found the sound muted, as if his fingers were gloved. The gray ceiling tiles must have been sound dampening.

What's quieter, he thought, an art gallery or a tomb? Until now he'd not staked out either. Cole sat on one of the room's three padded benches. Under other circumstances there'd be people sitting around with sketchbooks making intent studies. A horrible way to spend the day to Cole's

21

way of thinking. Cole hunched forward and closed his eyes, letting the quiet and solitude heighten his senses. He heard his heartbeat and the woman's slight respiration. There was a sense that if he could immerse himself a bit more in the silence then he'd become attuned to the voice that must be present. He strained forward, head cocked, seeking insinuations of a whisper.

What he instead heard were screams and choking coughs. The room was filled with people pleading as their flesh burned. Cole got up, shaking, shoving his hand into his coat pocket to grip the metal. The hallucination would not abate, painting itself over the present walls with brutal vividness. Smoke and chaos reduced him to helpless boyhood. "Dad! Dad!" he shouted and sought. He found the dais where his father stood beside the burning painting, one hand over his mouth, the other swatting at the flames with his dress jacket. Even now some dignitary, a member of Directorate, tried to thwart him. This surprised Cole. Yet another new detail. The man's actions, however, did not shock him at all. Why wouldn't some of the Directorate consider themselves burnt offerings on the holy altar of art? Cole shouted again, pleading as he reached the dais. Now Dad quit his efforts and jumped down. They found each other as the smoke blackened and thickened and the glass walls and ceiling ushered harsh sunlight into the final moments of their lives.

Distant, adult analysis told Cole this wasn't right. He'd never reached his father after the fire started. They'd lost each other to the panicked stampede. If they'd shouted each other's names the cries were overwhelmed by screams and the strange sounds of hands, feet, and even heads battering the glass walls while thousands gazed on the dying and answered with their own failed attempts to shatter the heavy panes.

The realization disconnected Cole from the hallucination without ending it. He was an adult again, moving through the horror like a lucid dreamer, all other concerns gone. His father stood there watching him. Maybe, Cole thought, this moment was a gift. A chance to make reality different in his head. Dad's features were more detailed than Cole thought possible, from the sweat on his brow to the little bit of brown hair near his Adam's apple which his razor blade always missed. Cole was a grown man now finding evidence of himself in his dad's face. Like his father, Cole's sideburns began to curl three weeks after a haircut. And they had the same blue eyes. There was another similarity, something about the shared shape of their mouths, unnoticed in any photograph Cole had. Were these observations and the wonder and peace that accompanied them what Mikey had promised? He could have been content—would have been content—to just meditate on them. But Dad smiled and said, "I know a way out of here. Follow me, Cole."

He offered his hand.

Cole almost took it. But his right hand was still in his coat pocket, still gripping the metal, and instead he gripped harder and backed away.

"No," he said, shutting his eyes. "I can't believe I've let this happen. I've got a job to do. *Leave.*"

He made a mental push, as if to shove his father in the chest. The thought of it almost broke him but he persevered. In the next instant, Cole found himself standing in front of Susan Wills, so close his nose almost touched her forehead. He jumped back like she'd hissed at him and spun around to face the painting. It seemed tilted just then, ready to fall over. Bivvens' eyes seemed brighter than before, the acrylic paint reflecting more than the room's steady light. The lips offered no trace of mirth. It occurred to Cole the founder had not submitted to any impulse of vanity other than, perhaps, the sheer size of the canvas. Otherwise the portrait cataloged too many painful details. The forehead was too high and plagued by psoriasis. The nose, eyes and mouth were far too small in comparison, like a framed image from a distorting funhouse mirror. The hair, though dark, was sparse and unkempt, and felt torn out rather than lost. His was the only clean-shaven portrait, and he might have done better with a beard.

Okay, amateur hour's gone on about twenty minutes too long, he told himself, taking his hand from his pocket.

It was time to work.

He used his phone to photograph and take videos of Susan Wills and the painting from every angle. He took distance measurements and found the woman was standing right at six feet from the artwork.

Cole returned to the bench and started tapping notes into his phone. But distraction crept into his thoughts again. Amateur hour wanted overtime. He switched tasks and sent a text message to Mikey. *Where did you go? The dream's turning into a hallucination. Got to help me.*

He held the phone between his knees, waiting several minutes for a response that didn't come. He sent another text, one guaranteed to make him answer.

I'm going to end up in Midnight Village tonight. Pretty sure about it.

If Mikey saw that message and *could* respond, he would—right away. That had been the case since they met a year and a half ago.

Nothing.

Maybe he's at the bakery, Cole thought. He couldn't touch his phone at work.

Yeah, that made the most sense.

When nothing made much sense.

Cole put the phone away and turned his attention to Susan Wills.

What if she never moves?

The question didn't help his current perception of time. Every second had become a sweaty slog. Susan Wills stood there like some invincible old rock jutting out of the sea, braving whole lifetimes in the crashing waves of hours. Cole arched his back and wriggled inside his clothes, growing ever more aware he'd not showered this morning. His hair felt heavy with oil, like a dirty beanie he couldn't doff.

"*Something* happen," he said, and began pacing the room. He felt like he belonged to an uninspired mule team trudging the same rutted, circular path. This was the worst part of detective work, the waiting. It wasn't any different than sitting in a car waiting to photograph a client's husband leaving a hotel, but *damn,* a tumorous tediousness seemed to be swelling in his bone marrow worse than any boredom he'd ever experienced. Cole was halfway willing to return half his consulting fee if it'd get Susan Wills to move.

When Dimwitter returned at last, Cole was sitting on the bench nearest the woman, head hanging, on the verge of a catatonic state himself. The director's footsteps shocked him into alertness, and he got up.

"So sorry to be away so long. Meetings all day. Has anything . . . changed?"

"No," Cole said, fighting off a yawn. Susan Wills stood as stalwart as any dedicated guard.

"The gallery just closed."

"I didn't realize so much time had passed. I feel like I only just sat down to make notes."

"I suppose I should call for an ambulance. I don't see any other practical option."

"If you do that and let them take her away, you'll just be in the same situation you were before."

"But she won't be our responsibility any further."

"I understand your position. My own hasn't changed. This pattern will keep repeating until we discover what's causing it. That adds up to many more cases like Ms. Wills. Sooner or later, word is going to get out. Not the publicity the Directorate needs."

Dimwitter looked at the floor and gave the barest nod of agreement.

"I can't stay," he said.

"Don't need you to. It's what you're paying me to do. Just don't set the alarm on your way out."

"How can I thank you for waiting this out, Mr. Sharpe?"

"You can order me a pizza."

"I'll have the security guard do it now."

"Will he be staying?"

"Of course, it's his job. Isn't it for the best if someone else is in the building in case—*something happens*?"

"I suppose," Cole said. "But I still don't want him coming into this room."

"I'll tell him not to interfere. Thank you again for everything you're doing, Mr. Sharpe. This is all so unsettling."

Dimwitter offered his hand and Cole shook it.

"With luck we may know something by tomorrow. If not answers, then at least clues. Don't worry, I'm sure we'll both be gone by . . . "

"Mr. Sharpe?"

"Morning," Cole said, fighting off a little shiver.

Dimwitter gave him an uncertain look and excused himself. Cole watched him go and then turned to Susan Wills.

"It's 6:30 now. Sunset is 7:15. I have an uncanny feeling you're going to start moving once it's night. Care to make a bet?"

He held out his hand to her. She went on staring at the portrait.

Cole propped himself into the far-left corner and waited. Time no longer felt antagonistic or stubborn. The minutes were speeding along, lubricated by anticipation. He imagined the light dwindling beyond the spires of the Crayon Box leaving a sky of reds, pink, and purple rivaling any mountainous alpenglow. He imagined the hundreds of artists with their easels racing to capture it all on canvas, for such were the passions of the majority in New Florence, and such were their economies.

The woman jerked like a mannequin animating. Cole flinched to attention and stepped forward as she rotated toward the exit, her expression still vacant. He hurried closer, phone out recording footage.

"Ms. Wills, do you hear me?"

He heard something like a growl. It was his own stomach, and he pocketed his phone to concentrate on following the woman, whose departure was more direct than her arrival. As she entered the lobby, the guard was already standing at the doors as if he couldn't decide whether to open them for her or block them.

"Move aside," Cole said.

"What the hell's wrong with her?"

"No clue. Just be glad she's almost out of your hair."

"What about you?"

"I'm going to follow her."

"See where she goes?"

"That's the usual definition."

Susan Wills walked into the door and rebounded a few steps. This fascinated Cole. Was she oblivious to her environment? What was she seeing? He reached and pushed the door open, and she exited.

"Good luck," the guard said and pointed at a car in the distance. "Oh, there's the pizza. Guess I'll have to eat it."

A teenager walked up and double checked the address. "That's for me," Cole said, taking the box without breaking stride. The guard grumbled behind him, but he and the museum were already out of Cole's thoughts, his pulse and pace quickening as he anticipated the pursuit. Susan Wills walked with a steady gait, canted forward, a bit like some dedicated speed walker. Her purposeful stride reinforced Cole's earlier impression she was a lawyer or executive. In another context, he could have been tailing her on the way to a business lunch.

Cole ate a slice of pizza for some much-needed fuel. After thirty minutes of walking, they were nearing the outskirts of downtown proper. The northwestern shore of the city's great public lake, Florenzia, was coming into view. It too was planned art, modeled after Montana's Lake McDonald, 150 acres of clear water whose bed was a treasure trove of imported argillite stones. Decades of iron infusions had given the stones an astonishing array of colors, soft reds and sharp greens, oranges and purples and blues. Children called it Easter Egg Lake. The Crayon Box, closer than it seemed, rose on the opposite side to the southeast. The financial district could be reached on foot from here in another thirty minutes.

Cole assumed Susan Wills would be heading downtown. Her sudden left turn onto the Avenue of Colors threw him. This was New Florence's 25-mile-long pedestrian beltway, where more chalk drawings abounded and the LED bulbs in every streetlamp had an alternate tint. Couples strolled through and participated in kaleidoscope patterns on their way to some new rendezvous. Their languid pace was at odds with Susan Wills's determined stride, though she had nothing on the occasional joggers in black leggings and fleece who left locomotive white gusts of breath in their wake as they practiced the tiresome art of physical fitness regardless of temperature. Cole wanted to hurl slices of pizza at them.

My God, he thought. She *is* going into Midnight Village.

He'd followed Mikey down this same path six months ago, hired by a client for murky reasons, claims of theft without any evidence. *"Look, it doesn't matter. I'm paying you. Just follow him and tell me where he goes, okay?"*

It'd been the longest, most random stakeout ever. Mikey spent half the day shopping, coming out of stores with bags of goods he'd then just leave on street corners before moving on. He went so fast Cole had little time to stop and check the contents of the bags, finding shirts and pants, suggestive underwear. Mikey spent an hour eating in a fast-food place, then he walked up to a portrait artist in the financial district. Cole saw him touch the man on the back of the head and whisper into his ear. A moment later, the men were shaking hands and Mikey stood before him, affecting a ridiculous pose, arms crossed at the chest, head held high and noble. The artist worked fast but it was still a two-hour process, and in the end, Mikey took the canvas and put it in the nearest trash can.

"Sure, I knew you were there. The whole time. And you looked fine as hell, so I decided to show off a little bit. Went all peacock on you."

Then, at nightfall, Mikey got on the Avenue of Color and started heading northwest.

Cole dropped the pizza box and took out his phone.

Mikey, I'm heading into Midnight Village. No choice in the matter. Need my passport.

No response.

"Goddamnit," Cole said.

Susan Wills would reach *the spot* in just fifteen minutes. Cole glanced behind him to make certain of his bearings. The Crayon Box was behind them now, its bright colors subdued into pleasing pastels under moonlight. Just as they'd been when Mikey reached *the spot* and Cole's horizons were expanded in an instant. He could see it in his memory, the intersection—the doorway—the subtle shimmer in the air that led to Midnight Village. It existed down a simple path off to the right that led to a few empty park benches.

He sent Mikey another text. As urgent a message as he'd ever sent.

Need passport.

Still no reply.

Susan Wills took the little path toward the benches. The shimmer was there like a pocket of separate reality. Soon she'd pass through it just as Mikey had. Mikey had been surprised Cole could follow him through it when he confronted Cole on the other side, standing there with a dangerous little smile as he watched Cole try to reorient himself to a vast and immediate change in environment.

29

The vibrant streetlights were gone, replaced with sodium lamp yellow, the color of a sick man's urine. The Crayon Box stood at the same distance, but it was all ash and gray like some gravestone charcoal rubbing.

"Don't think you should be here, handsome."

"Where am I?"

"The place parents have in mind when they tell their kids to stay away from something. Even if they don't realize it. The locals call it Midnight Village."

"What locals? I don't see anyone around but you."

"That's because we're on the very edge of town. Plenty of things to interest a tourist—if there were such a thing— but the population density isn't hanging out around here."

"How did I get here?"

"Thought you were a detective. The obvious answer is you were following me and I led you in."

"Then how did you get here?"

"There's two ways from what I can tell. You've either made a demonic pact—"

"What?"

"Or you were born with a little extra."

"Extra?"

"Something special about you. A natural ability no one else has. I'm just assuming here. I'm the only mind reader around as far as I know. I stumbled into the place a few years ago and learned I could come and go as I please. Everyone else I've met sold their souls for admission."

As Cole watched Susan Wills nearing the shimmer, he started to slow. I can't, he thought. Can't follow without a passport.

"Look in the sky. Those dark shapes are wraiths. They're quite keen to destroy you. I can read their desire even from here. But they won't because you're with me. My extra has you covered like an umbrella. This is a new discovery for me. Want to see more? If so, then consider

me your living, breathing, very fuckable passport to Midnight Village."

She was heading straight for the shimmer. Thinking of the wraiths, Cole gave up any pretense of following her and ran up to grab her shoulder. No force could restrain her. She shook him off without any notice.

"What's Midnight Village? Think of it like a trip on the Dark Web. It exists right alongside what's visible but it's unseen and inaccessible. You're experiencing the unindexed life now, handsome. You got the extra, you got the browser. Go where you like. See what you'll see."

Susan Wills reached the threshold of the shimmer and passed through. Cole stopped. Goddamnit. He texted Mikey one more time.

No choice. MV now. Begging you.

Beyond the shimmer, Susan Wills kept walking. She was disappearing fast, becoming indistinct and discolored like a smear of cigarette ash across a sepia photograph.

Can't lose her, Cole told himself. Come on, Mikey, don't let me down.

"So, what's extra about you besides those bright blue eyes?"

"I don't know."

"Did you sell your soul to the Devil for those good looks?"

"No."

"What about prophetic visions? Premonitions? Ever have those?"

"I get bad dreams sometimes."

"I wouldn't mind giving you some good ones. Sure you don't have any extra?"

"Pretty sure."

"You reek of tragedy. Ghosts are currency in Midnight Village. Maybe you've got a few Caspers hugging your balls. Lucky ghosts."

Cole gripped the metal in his coat pocket as he passed through the shimmer. He stepped into a different city, a

31

mix of contemporary New Florence and something far older, New Florence as it might look if architectural standards, materials, and sensibilities never progressed beyond 1850. Everywhere a curious mix of brick and wood. The air was colder, sharper, with a wet bite like autumn drizzle, though it was all quite dry. A hint of mist further off, as the unmarked street wound toward a collection of blighted neo-Classical buildings, every window shattered but candelabras burning on the sills. Susan Wills was moving down that path. He saw no one else anywhere. He cast a worried glance up. Dark, shrieking shapes circled in the black sky like a growing kettle of vultures.

Cole turned, determined to dive back onto the Avenue of Color. But the shimmer was gone.

More shrieks. More circling shapes, descending.

Desperation fed a starved muse. He bolted ahead toward Susan Wills and forced his left arm into the bend of her right elbow. The wraiths had ignored her. The force that brought her here was serving as a passport. Maybe he could borrow its safety.

He looked up again. Never mind us, he thought. We're just two lovers on a stroll through Damnation Alley.

Cole almost stumbled and looked ahead of him, feeling the tug of whatever compelled the woman forward like an invisible rope around her waist.

The first wraith dropped about a hundred yards ahead of them. More bleak, elongated forms followed, silent darts seeking their bullseye. Fourteen all together. They seemed to have no weight at all, their bodies gesticulating like a platoon of air dancers meant to draw the eye to some new corner car wash or pizzeria. If you just stared at them there was no hint of forward motion, yet every eyeblink disclosed a grim and inexorable progress, like mutilated mimes under a strobe light. Their spindly, flailing arms stretched closer and closer.

Cole gripped the metal tighter and tighter but even the fiercest clutching couldn't restore his failing nerve. The wraiths sponged away his courage, an aperitif before the main course of his flesh. Susan Wills was taking him straight toward them and he tore himself free and ran for the imagined safety of the ruined buildings, the burning candles. The wraiths had closed off every escape. Their lurid, silent gesticulations made Cole think he was some poor fish trying to navigate through a thousand stinging anemones.

He fell to his knees, crushed by the weight of futility. The glass gallery started forming around him before he quite realized he was summoning it, determined to spend his final moments here.

Cole stood up, finding no sign of wraiths or Susan Wills or Midnight Village, just the fire on all sides, and men and women blackening on the floor, their expensive suits and coats fuel for flame.

"Dad?" he said, stepping over the bodies. His father stood on the dais next to the painting, which was framed in fire. The canvas was not burning. Dad was staring at it in a way that reminded him of Susan Wills.

Cole tried to climb the dais, but it was too hot to touch. He shouted and waved but his father gave no indication of hearing him.

"I should have died in the fire with you. It was wrong that I didn't. Maybe we'd be hanging out in the afterlife with Mom. Instead, I got a reprieve, and I didn't do jack shit with it to make a difference. Maybe I'll end up in Hell. I bet Hell is having to stand still forever in front of an ugly painting."

Cole's gaze shifted to the canvas and its burning frame. There was no image. At first, he thought the fire must have melted the painting, but no: the canvas was white and pure.

"That's not right," he said, not sure why the blankness bothered him. He tried to pull the right details from memory in the little time he had left.

His father's voice startled him out of the effort.

"If we hadn't panicked when the painting started to burn, we could have put out the fire with our combined gaze."

"Dad?"

"Isn't that what a painting needs, Cole? To be seen? To be studied?"

The wraiths appeared outside the glass walls, their reality intruding on the dream at last. Cole fought against choking up as he looked back to his father.

"Love you, Dad. I've tried to do okay without you, but you'd be disappointed in me. I want to show you one last thing. It's all the magic I have in my life, and I owe it to you."

He started to pull the metal from his coat. Before he could, though, his father's form turned into pure, cold blackness, stretched tall and thin, and his lengthening arms began to whip and lash at Cole's body. Cole shut his eyes tight, hugging himself as he thought: Please don't be too painful, please—

"Back away, you damn vultures. Get your meat somewhere else. This one's with me."

Mikey's voice shattered all traces of the dream. Cole found himself in a tight ring of wraiths, their blackness seeping over his skin with a feeling like cold latex paint. They weren't backing off.

Mikey forced his way into the middle and raised his right hand.

"Mr. Passport has arrived. Sorry boys, he's with me and you all can go back to your magic carpet ride in the sky."

The circle of wraiths widened bit by bit, a begrudging retreat. Cole tried to speak but found his teeth chattering. Too many parts of his body radiated a cold fury. He managed to look at Mikey's face and found an expression that could have fit an army medic looking at a dying soldier. He bent and wrapped his arms around Cole's shoulders and started pulling him up. Cole found he had no sensation in his feet. His legs were plunged into a black pool. Though Mikey stood three inches shorter than Cole, he wrapped him in a bear hug and gave three impressive heaves that hoisted Cole free like a man pulled from quicksand.

"You okay?"

"I'm freezing," Cole managed. "Can't feel—"

"Say no more. It's wraith poisoning. A bartender friend of mine told me about it a few months ago. Wanted to warn me in case I ever got attacked. Pretty presumptuous of him. If you haven't sold your soul to the Devil, you're sort of a second-class citizen around here. Viewed as wraith food waiting to happen. He mentioned being able to brew up an antidote. Can you make it about twenty blocks?"

Cole nodded without conviction. He took one step and started to collapse. His legs weren't even stilts. They were air. Mikey got a shoulder under him to keep him upright. "Lean on me," he said, breaking into song. "When you're not strong. First get you well, and then we'll fuck later on . . . "

Susan Wills was long gone, impossible to track, but Mikey was unfeeling about it as Cole filled him in on what happened.

"Where the hell have you been? Whatever you did has turned the dream into a waking hallucination. I've been fighting it all day."

"Unforeseen complications," Mikey said.

"Do you mean what I'm experiencing or why you left?"

"Would you quit asking twenty questions while I'm dragging your ass across Midnight Village—to save your life, I might add."

They came to a brick building covered in gray, wilted moss. A red tavern door, heavy wood with a rounded arch, stood ajar a few inches. Mikey pulled it open, and Cole limped into a space from the Middle Ages, with five long, empty communal tables served by a single barkeep, a tall and lean man with sparse blonde hair like brittle autumn sedge. He had an easel set up in the darkened corner. The canvas was just a mess of black paint.

"Hell, Dan, not you too," Mikey said as he eased Cole down on the end of a bench.

The bartender put his brush and palette down. "Guilty as charged."

"I thought you said mixology was the truest art."

"I used to believe that. Sold my soul to master it. But painting is the fast track to permanent citizenship. Who's this?"

"A buddy. Hope you weren't lying about that wraith medicine."

Cole tried to focus on the man's face. He didn't like the expression he saw.

"Not lying, no. But it's not tested."

"Goddamnit," Mikey said.

"I'm sure it will work," the bartender said, coming over to peer at Cole. "Just have to tailor it to the individual. Faith is the key ingredient. What's your religion?"

"I don't have one."

He rolled his eyes and Mikey prodded Cole for a better answer. "How were you raised?"

"Dad never went to church after Mom died."

"Where did you go when she was alive?"

"I think it was Methodist. Hell, I don't know."

Mikey looked at the bartender. "Can you make a brew for *general Christianity?*"

"We'll just do Catholicism."

The bartender turned and started pulling from the rows of bottles behind him. He mixed, shook, and stirred, adding things that looked like olives which caught fire once they touched liquid. This went on for several minutes, all the while a chill spread through Cole's thighs. Mikey cupped one hand behind Cole's head and gave him a reassuring rub.

The bartender came over with a small pitcher and three plastic cups on a tray. He poured a rust-colored concoction to each brim and pushed the first cup toward Cole. Black flecks floated in the brown water. Then he turned and went back to the corner to resume painting.

"I'm not drinking that."

"You better," the bartender said. "And quick, before it sets and thickens."

"I'm not Catholic."

"Let me remind you of the situation, handsome. Drink this or die."

"Like I said, I'm not—"

"Catholic means universal," the bartender said. "In Midnight Village it's the negative-O blood type of religions."

"Right," Mikey said. "Now hoover up the blood of Christ before it gets so thick you have to chew it."

Cole would have kept resisting but another cold spike drove north into his groin. He reached for the first cup, closed his eyes, and tilted his head back. When the liquid didn't hit his tongue right away, he started to pull back. Mikey prevented him. It took half a minute before the contents slid into his mouth like some goaded slug.

As Cole coughed and tried to swallow, Mikey said, "I told you to be quick about it. The next two are going to be even worse."

Cole shuddered even as he worked at swallowing the first dose. The liquid made a hard place in his esophagus. He gulped again, massaging the base of his throat and the substance cleared. He swore he felt it drop straight into his stomach like a stone pitched into a pond. He gasped a moment, getting ready to demand answers.

"Don't try talking right now. Just focus on swallowing the rest of the Blood of Christ."

Cole shook his head and pressed his lips tight as Mikey held up the next cup.

"Isn't one good enough?"

"Do you feel better?"

37

"Yes."

"Liar," Mikey said. "You're in this situation because you made a dumb mistake. Don't double down on another."

"I'm in this situation because *you* didn't—"

"Wow, that's *dense*," Mikey said, tilting the cup back and forth. The contents made the slightest shift.

Cole took the cup and turned it upside down above his wide-open mouth. He tapped the bottom and waited. What fell onto his tongue had the texture of a cupcake, the taste of raw flesh. Cole began chewing.

"I had to get out of your apartment. I didn't want to go. The power of your dream started to infect me. For a moment there, I almost became you as you were, watching those people burn. I left to save myself. I thought I could shake the dream once I was away, but that didn't quite happen. I've still got a little bit of it stuck between my ears."

Cole kept chewing as he listened. The taste had changed from raw flesh to notes of rusty coffee tins and creepy crawlies. He'd eaten worms and bugs as a child and you never forgot that gritty earthen smack. He reached for the third cup in anticipation. There was no give to it. The liquid had turned into a substance resembling hardened Playdough. He picked at the top crust and brought a few flecks to his lips.

"I should come clean on something, Cole. From the moment you told me you survived that fire, I started wondering if there was another reason you were able to follow me into Midnight Village. Because *Gone By Morning* is still a big deal here."

"What does that exhibit have to do with—"

He noticed the bartender was now staring at him with great, open intensity, until Cole couldn't stand it anymore. *"What?"*

The bartender turned to Mikey. "This guy knows Fangsy?"

Cole laughed. "What the *fuck* is a Fangsy?"

The bartender and Mikey gave the room a worried *sound travels* look.

"A vampire," Mikey said, hushed. Cole blinked at him, quite certain he'd heard right and quite certain he couldn't believe it.

"I've got a guy who knows Fangsy in my bar? Do you think he could put in a word? My painting skills aren't very good yet, I know that, but—"

"I'm sure he can. He owes you his life, after all."

Mikey cast a knowing glance at Cole, who played along without a clue of comprehension. "Happy to do it."

The bartender ran back to the canvas and said, "This can be a masterpiece by the time I'm done. Worthy of citizenship. But it doesn't have a name. Names are important. A great painting has to have a memorable name, like *Gone By Sunrise*—"

"Call it *The Gift of Night*."

The bartender's eyes and smile brightened in unison. "I was thinking of titling it that."

"You don't say? Better get back to work on it, Dan. Cole, how are you doing? Ready for a walk?"

"I am," Cole said.

"Then we'll be on our way. Thanks again, Dan. I bet you'll be hearing from Fangsy in a few days. Trust me."

"I don't have the words," the bartender said, shaking Cole's hand. His eyes were weepy.

Cole followed Mikey out the door, back to the lonesome street. The bartender's hopeful aspiration lingered in his thoughts.

"What was all that citizenship stuff about?"

"Standard definition, handsome. Living here full time. Dedicating yourself to its culture."

"What culture?"

"Fangsy's," Mikey said. This time the name didn't sound as silly.

"So vampires are real?"

"One is, at least."

"Who is he? You said the gallery fire is a big deal in Midnight Village. What's it to anyone here?"

Mikey was silent a moment. "We're both children of New Florence. What does that mean to you?"

"That I'm supposed to love art. Worship it. Practice it every waking moment of my life. Tithe to the Directorate on Sundays."

"Midnight Village is just the same way. But there is no Directorate, there's just Fangsy. He can decide if you live or die around here. If you want to stay, you have to do art, and you have to do art that pleases him."

"So what pleases him?"

Mikey looked up. "Night skies. Blood moons. A good eye for composition."

"Be serious, for Christ's sake!"

"I am being serious. If you really want to understand Midnight Village, you've got to understand Fangsy. He *is* Midnight Village, and New Florence was Midnight Village before it was New Florence."

"You're not making any sense, Mikey."

"So once there was this little artist's colony with fifteen members."

"I know the story."

"Do you? Something happened. Call it a split. A split in reality but another kind too, like when a fertilized egg splits and you get twins. Two cities, two realities. But it's also a case of vanishing twins, like when one baby eats the other in the womb. The former's somewhere in the latter. But is Midnight Village in New Florence or is New Florence in Midnight Village? Question for the philosophers."

"So what's Fangsy? The father?"

"Father, founder, use whatever word you like," Mikey said.

"Have you ever met him?"

"Hell no. Haven't even seen him."

"But he's here somewhere in Midnight Village?"

"Downtown. The lower levels. Nowhere I want to go."

"I do," Cole said.

Mikey shook his head. "There's Midnight Village and then there's *Midnight Village*. My *extra* lets me walk around but when it comes down to it, I'm just a tourist. Happy to skim the surface. When it comes to Fangsy, we're talking about getting down to bone marrow."

"Fine," Cole said.

Mikey laughed. "*Fine?*"

"I'm not here as a tourist. I have a job to do. Locate Susan Wills. Find out what's going on with the galleries. That means getting my hands dirty."

"You really don't know what you're talking about—"

Cole grabbed Mikey by the shoulders and shook him, shouting, "Is he responsible for the fire that killed my dad?" For a moment he couldn't even see Mikey's face through a haze of red.

Mikey was silent, his eyes wide and a little wet. Cole let go of him and apologized.

"I want to find Fangsy because I'm betting Susan Wills is with him. This isn't about me. It's about the case."

"Sure it is, handsome," Mikey said. "Sure it is."

The pavement shifted to a sudden and steep declining grade, so much so that Cole thought he was going to fall forward. By all other appearances they were almost in New Florence's financial district. The Crayon Box, stripped of color, loomed overhead. But no street in the city made such a descent. He felt like he was going down a mine shaft.

"Guess it's fitting," Mikey said after not talking for twenty minutes.

"What?"

"A baker making himself toast."

"What do you have to worry about? You've got the *extra*."

"Don't mean nothing in this part of Midnight Village.

We're about to get down to where the real residents live. The tribe of true artists Dan wants to join. Some guy who can read thoughts and do a few mind tricks doesn't even register with them. That may be a good thing. Better to go unnoticed."

There were no streetlamps anymore, no clear source of ambient light anywhere. Dusk light nevertheless prevailed, and under its glow Cole saw a change in the sidewalk that made him groan. Chalk drawings.

"Even here?"

Cole, who thought nothing of stepping on them in New Florence, started to put his foot down when Mikey yanked him onto the street.

"Let's *not* do that."

"It's just some kid's drawings."

"You better check again."

They walked on the road parallel to the sidewalk. The drawings kept going, each square an expert depiction of something vile. War and slaughter. Torture. Cole saw no immediate connection between the squares, but after a few more steps, he detected a continuous narrative. An ancient story, sinister and sorrowful.

"It's like someone did the Bayeaux tapestry as chalk art."

"I don't know the entire story or the history or how it all ties in, but I'm told the piece is called *The Education of the Innocents*."

Cole stooped and angled himself to see better, as each image was upside down from his position. On the immediate square before him, two women had been stripped naked and raped by men in monk's robes. More men stood around them. Erect crucifixes rose from their crotches.

"I've also heard it called *How Sacred Art Entered the World*."

Cole stood up. "Sacred art? Painting?"

"Hate," Mikey said. "The women are Solseanna and Marquierta. I think I've got their names right. They were witches and sisters. Maybe lovers. Or both. They could have been people like me, born with abilities no one could understand. Their powers brought them unwanted attention, as you can see."

"The rape."

"Rapes," Mikey said. "You'll find a lot of variations on this square as we keep going. I figure the story passes about a decade for every five squares. Rape after rape and child after child, each angrier than the next. Hating their mothers, hating their unknown fathers, hating their prisons of flesh and bone, soil and rock. They'll become a tribe of their own, masters and practitioners of hate— hence the sacred art."

Cole grunted. "So one of them is Fangsy?"

"More like ancient ancestors. Assuming it's not just artistic mythological bullshit. Artists here are like artists anywhere, only more so. Self-aggrandizement out the ass."

"Where *are* the artists?"

Mikey pointed ahead of them. "If we keep going down this road, we'll start seeing them. Not just painters, either. Musicians, sculptors. I've never gone far enough down to see the sculptors. The painters do a pretty good job of freaking me out."

"Why?"

"You'll see. With luck they'll be lost in their work but be prepared to run if they're looking for a model."

Cole reached into his coat pocket. Touched the metal. Mikey glanced at the motion.

They moved forward, buffeted now by a steady, sharp breeze that smelled of petrichor and minerals, as if flavored from the mouth of a cave. The dusk light persisted, and the chalk drawings were now the same repeated image—a person walking alone. Sometimes the figure's background changed from mountains to forests to open skies. The traveler continued and Cole lost himself in following the progress, so very much like the individual cells of a flipbook animation.

"There they are," Mikey said.

Cole turned his attention to the road. Not far off, the way seemed blocked by hundreds of figures, a haze of people standing or sitting by turns in postures familiar to anyone from New Florence. He thought of all the times he walked near the Crayon Box, moving among the happy artists stationed before some tree, building, or person with their easels out, canvases mounted, paintbrush in hand. Here were their mirror figures, a population of phantasms standing before easels, every canvas black, their color palettes various shades of ash except for one peculiar, garish red, the color of roses dying in lapels.

"We're just going to tiptoe around them but remember what I said. If anyone seems to be looking for a model, start running."

Cole nodded, but he was only half-listening. He'd gotten close enough to see the image on the nearest canvas. The spectral painter took no notice and consulted no model as their paintbrush fleshed out a scene in grim, expert strokes. Cole saw a car idling on a lonely road, the world streaked with rain. He found the image taking hold of his mind, transporting him. For a moment, Cole stood at the back of the car, breathing the damp air, watching the brake lights flare against the gray and black night. His hand eased into his coat pocket to grip the metal, directed by a despair he couldn't pinpoint. Something terrible was about to happen. He needed to open the driver's side door. Needed to prevent a tragedy. But on his first step forward, a gunshot made him flinch and gasp.

Cole blinked. He was standing in Midnight Village again, watching the artist work. His merciless paintbrush made a cruel red slash across the back window of the car. Cole felt it like a cut in his skin.

Mikey put a hand on his shoulder. "I didn't bother telling you not to look. I knew you'd have to look."

"Suicide on a lonesome road."

"Great title. Right up there with *Nighthawks*."

"I feel like the painting just made it happen—somewhere."

He shivered and felt Mikey's hand on the small of his back.

"This is what Dan wants to become. They're all students of Fangsy's. Souls who paint scenes to trouble dreamers. Each canvas is someone's sleeping mind. Someone's unconscious state. Someone's night terror."

Cole looked at his feet.

"Think any of them ever painted *my* dream?"

"I wish that's all your dream was," Mikey said, and in the next instant Cole found himself being kissed with more intensity than he'd ever experienced. Passion and compassion all at once, a kiss meant to heal. Mikey's eyes were wide open and Cole looked into them, wondering if this kiss could be an act of defiance against the nightmares flourishing all around them. Did the painters notice?

Mikey pulled back, his smile mischievous, his eyes earnest. "Let's get out of here. Give up the case. Go back to your apartment and we'll pick a new future together from a big deck of Tarot cards."

Cole looked ahead, unable to see further down the road but knowing there was more to go. More to go ever and always. He couldn't kid himself. It wasn't about Susan Wills or the case now. It wasn't even about some shadowy character named Fangsy. His father was the sort of man who always wanted to see what was around the bend. His father would already be a mile down the road by now.

Mikey frowned. "I'm not liking your thoughts, handsome."

"I know."

He let Mikey lead him through the maze of painters, careful not to provoke or jostle. Cole forced himself to confront the profound sorrows rendered in gray and black on each passing canvas. Their models were abused children left alone in foreign places on icy nights. Victims

45

of gun violence, victims of home invasions and intimidation and threat. Their landscapes showed storm clouds building over desolate plains, bloody raindrops. The painters studied expressions of grief in minute detail, capturing moments of dark realization—the Stage 4 cancer diagnosis, the betrayed spouse, the parents present to see their child's body dredged from a lake.

His jaw hurt from clenching as they got clear of that crowd. The next group of artists offered no relief, and now the street verged on the point of impassibility. Violinists and cellists, flautists, guitarists, trumpeters, and drummers made bleak ensembles gathered in a dense profusion. Their collective noise should have deafened, but it rose to the level of a cold wind's whistle, the crack and rustling of dead leaves, the whimpers and dry pleading behind hospice room doors. Songs as hollow as prayers to an unbelieved god. Choral soloists added tubercular coughs for chants, and hooded figures carried bone wind chimes dangling from sticks that made ancient tribal murmurings.

Mikey, standing ahead of Cole, pivoted to face him. Fascination showed in his eyes. "You've heard this before—"

Then Mikey was gone and so was the street. Cole stood in the glass gallery again and he heard the song of the musicians in the screams of the dying. This detail was new and true, not some sudden addition to a hallucination but a recovered memory. The song was in the people begging for their lives, it was in the hacking coughs and the efforts to shatter the walls. On the other side of the smoky glass, he saw police officers drawing guns and shooting point blank. The gallery reduced their powerful bullets to BBs, the song also in the *ping, ping* of their harmless ricochets.

Dead bodies stood up all around him. Cole saw they were the musicians, engulfed in flames. The song came from the center of their chests, pushing him like a physical thing. His hand dug for the metal even as he staggered toward the front of the gallery. The musicians gathered behind him, the smell and sound of their burning flesh all part of their song. Cole saw his father standing alone on the dais, arms aloft, motioning like a conductor. His bloodless face bore a strange expression, his eyes glittering and obsessed. A heresiarch on the verge of seeing his heresy conquer the old order. No trace of the man Cole remembered, no trace of his father *as he'd been*. His arms moved with ever greater urgency, directing the song, gathering it, raising it toward the roof.

That's not Dad, Cole thought. This isn't my dream anymore. It's something—*extra*.

"Mikey? If you can hear me, I need your help."

He squeezed the metal harder than ever. Its rounded form was not sharp, but he gripped until its dull edges cut his skin. He showed his bleeding palm to the musicians.

"Will this make you quit?"

He turned and waved his bloody hand at his father.

"Is this what you want?"

His father's movements came to a lifeless stop. Cole now realized there was a shadowy figure lurking behind him. Blue fingers, thin as ribbons, curled about each wrist, conducting the conductor on the fantoccini stage. Like a metastasizing growth, a second head emerged to the right of his father's, its pate as blue as a drowning victim's, with mottled black bruises and eyes and lips as red as the paint on the palettes of the horror artists they'd harrowed. The corners of the mouth had strange growths drooping off them like layers of argyria rose petal tumors and his instant disgust at the sight kept his own stare directed up at the creature's eyes. Their gaze seemed to lasso his bleeding hand, and a slip of black tongue wetted the crimson lips.

His father was cast aside and landed with a mannequin hollowness. The revealed maestro had fingers as long as paintbrushes and pointed nails like bristles wetted into little spears. Cole did not understand how its toothless smile could be so biting, but he felt some chunk of himself torn out when he saw it. The musicians fell silent. Even the flames made no noise.

The figure strode across the dais, gave Cole a look of contempt, and swiped his right hand across the blank framed canvas. The paper ripped open like a fat man's stomach, guts and viscera spilling out from the savage tear as if some perpetual grinder existed on the other side to keep meat pumping through in ever thickening folds.

"My beautiful masterpiece," the figure said, sepulchral voiced and gloating as he drew himself up to his full, angular height like some blue praying mantis.

Cole backed away from the lava flow of flesh as it spilled off the dais. He passed through the musicians, all the way to the glass wall. As his shoulders bumped against it, the thing on the stage looked straight at him and whispered, *"Masterpiece, masterpiece."*

Hands came through the glass and wrapped around his waist. Cole shouted as he was pulled back through the wall. In the next instant he found himself on the street in Midnight Village, struggling to catch his breath as Mikey held him.

"You're okay now."

"I'm not sure about that."

"You went catatonic on me. Been trying to snap you out of it."

"The dream."

"I know."

Cole looked at him. "But *not* the dream. Not even a hallucination. Just . . . not what really happened."

Mikey went quiet with a grave expression too foreign for his face.

"You're wrong about that, Cole. It's like I said last night. The mind records everything that goes on but it seldom gives back all the details. My goal was to dredge it all up."

"Mikey, what I saw *didn't*—"

"*Everything,* even if the eyes and ears don't realize it. Everything that was present."

"There was a thing there. A monster. Standing behind my father."

"Fangsy."

"But he was toothless. How can he be a vampire? Why call himself Fangsy if—"

"There are many ways to draw blood, Cole. Don't underestimate anything about him. The dream proves he was there. His shadow. His spirit. His evil intent."

"The bastard called it a masterpiece. He didn't mean the painting. He was referring to Dad. To all the dead people. The drapes, the glass building—the whole thing was designed to show people dying before an audience like . . . like some piece of performance art."

"Remember the *sacred art*. Hate is his true practice."

"He's working on something new," Cole said. "Something that will make *Gone By Morning* seem trivial."

"You know that for sure?"

"I think the details of my case prove it. People like Susan Wills are going catatonic in front of paintings and then disappearing. They're answering Fangsy's call."

"To do what?"

Cole couldn't hazard an answer. He shook his head.

"This is going to be more than you can take on, handsome. More than you'd ever want to deal with."

"I've got to try."

"You can try punching a brick wall until it falls down, too. You're just going to end up with bloody knuckles."

Cole brought his right hand out of his pocket. His palm was wet and red just as it was in the dream. He must have been gripping the metal for all of its considerable worth.

"Looks like I'm halfway there," he said.

They slept together that night in Cole's apartment, a sleep of mutual protection, neither out of each other's touch very long. Cole's stretches of sleep were dreamless, and he'd jolt awake with a paranoid certainty Mikey had taken the dream. Without opening his eyes, Mikey would say, "I didn't." Then Cole would sink back onto the mattress and hold Mikey like some totem against the dark, a bit ashamed by his sudden infantilism, the fear of the monster at the window, the monster in the closet.

Red eyes. Red lips.

In the morning they showered and ate together, neither quite meeting the other's gaze and both almost silent. Cole was struck by how it felt like the morning after an awkward hookup and he didn't understand. It was on his mind as he poured them both a bowl of cereal and put a pod in the Keurig machine.

"You're feeling really chaotic now," Mikey said.

"Just how telepathic are you?"

"Depends."

"On what?"

"Physical attraction."

Cole smiled. "You being serious?"

"I am. My *extra* seemed to spring up with my boner. In high school, I could just sit behind the entire basketball team and hop back and forth between their heads, eavesdropping like a DEA agent tapping a phone line. Meanwhile I couldn't squeeze a single thought from one of the cheerleaders. You know how Superman can't see through lead? I guess women are my lead. I also can't read ugly guys for shit. But I think I could read your thoughts from miles away."

Cole sat the cereal bowls on the table. "Miles?"

"I remember sitting in a bar and noticing you outside the window. I figured you were just waiting for your girlfriend or something. Damn, he's cute, I told myself. And like that, your mind was open to me. Imagine my surprise when I realized what you were doing. So I decided to have some fun, just so I could hang out in your thoughts a little longer. Not a decision I've ever regretted."

Cole frowned a little as he took a seat. "I owe you a lot."

"I know."

"I mean I never really have thanked you for—"

"You just did."

They laughed. Mikey poured milk into the bowl.

"We should date," he said.

Cole nodded. "I was thinking about that."

"Maybe become business partners."

"What?"

"I've said it before. A private investigator with a genuine telepath as a sidekick? Pretty unbeatable team. And a much better use of my strengths than baking bread."

"I need to think about—"

Cole's cell phone buzzed. Dimwitter.

"I didn't make that happen," Mikey said.

Grinning, Cole answered the call.

"Mr. Sharpe, my name is Maurice Jampier. I'm Mr. Dimwitter's assistant."

"Yes?"

"Are you available to come to the Central Gallery right now?"

"Slow down. What's wrong?"

"It's another incident."

"Where's Dimwitter?"

A pause, then:

"He is the incident."

Cole shifted the phone to his other ear and looked at Mikey.

"He came up to the administrative offices on the top floor," Jampier continued. "Talked to me like usual and was mentioning how eager he was for an update from you. Then his expression went blank. He went down to the Grand Gala room. I followed him down and found him staring up at a painting. He wouldn't say a word to me."

"How long ago was this?"

"Maybe twenty minutes."

Cole told him to take no action until he arrived. This time he drove, racing out with just enough time to spare

Mikey a kiss goodbye. Mikey was already sending a resignation text to his boss.

"Don't get too far ahead of yourself," Cole said. "There's a lot to discuss."

Mikey just smiled.

The Central Gallery was right in the heart of the Crayon Box, too squat to be noticed in the skyline but present like the clasp of a belt holding everything together. Considering Jampier's anxiety, Cole expected to see police cars and ambulances surrounding the place. He found none as he entered the garage parking lot and hurried into the lobby. Central was the Directorate's crown jewel so Cole was surprised by the reduced foot traffic. Busloads of tourists were there in their usual abundance but few schoolchildren and teachers leading field trips. The only evidence of trouble were two security guards who seemed to be modeling tension along with their square jawlines.

"Mr. Sharpe?"

He turned. A man in his 40s, a bit plump and dressed in an ill-fitting blue suit, approached.

"Jampier?"

They didn't shake hands. Jampier guided Cole forward. In a low voice, he said, "I don't think anyone's noticed and we're trying to keep the matter low profile. Maybe we're blessed that the problem is happening in the Grand Gala. It's the hub of the whole building. So many people coming and going, no one takes much notice of others."

"Looks to be a slower day, too."

"That's because tomorrow is the Directorate's Free Day. Half the classrooms in the state will visit one of our galleries then."

"Well," Cole said. "I know where I won't be tomorrow."

They entered the Grand Gala room. It had the appearance of a rotunda, capped by a 30-foot dome ceiling made of intricate stained glass, shards of red, blue, and green that could be lit from behind during holidays, raining jigsaw patterns on the people whose upturned gazes sought celestial understanding in the planetarium of art. When not lit, as now, the crowds had to contend with the distraction of fifteen oil paintings whose scale made the self-portrait of Royland G. Bivvens seem wallet sized. Cole had not been in the room since childhood when the cathedral effect and gigantism awed him. Each work belonged to the Modernist school, Pollackian layers of paint splashed and drizzled in a dizzying extravagance. Sheer size made every canvas seem a window to the cosmos.

Cole had already identified Dimwitter from the back before Jampier pointed. He stood straight and still and silent, head inclined so that his stare was fixed on a painting called *The Lament*. Another man stood to Dimwitter's left and seemed to be conversing with him.

"One-sided conversation?"

"Mr. Dimwitter is an important man. We'll do everything we can to disguise his—misfortune."

"How much do you know about the other occurrences?"

"Everything up to yesterday morning."

Cole nodded, scanning the room. The Grand Gala could contain about 300 people if they all squeezed together. Right now, he saw less than half that number streaming in and out of the room's four doorways. People pushing strollers and wheelchairs. There was a marked difference between tourists seeing the room for the first time and locals who blew through it on their way to another exhibit. There seemed to be a lot of locals who weren't paying the paintings or Dimwitter much attention.

"What time do you close?"

"9PM."

"Ok. Based on what I've observed so far, I don't think he's in any immediate danger. He may not make any movement until tonight. No need to call for an ambulance."

"I thought we might move him—"

"*No.* Best to let this play out. If you're still worried

53

about appearances, we can just cycle people in and out to pretend to talk to him. No harm there. What I need from you right now is mission critical."

Jampier stiffened. "What can I do?"

"I need access to the security camera footage for this room for the last 24 hours. Maybe further out than that."

"I can arrange that."

Jampier motioned to another room attendant, who stepped over and began the awkward, thankless task of faking a conversation. Dimwitter swayed a little—more than Susan Wills had—but never stopped staring at *The Lament*.

The security room was on the top floor's administrative wing, the least artistic space Cole had ever seen. There wasn't so much as a cheap framed portrait on the walls of the short white hallways. Jampier led him to a gray door marked *Security*. An officer opened it from within and was instructed to provide whatever Cole needed. Then Jampier left.

They sat down in front of several rows of flat screen monitors. Two were marked *Grand Gala* and Cole was pleased by the initial view. Wide angles and detailed, expansive shots. Much better quality than the West gallery cameras. Dimwitter was easy to identify. One camera caught him from behind, the second showed him almost in profile.

The officer switched the first camera away from the live feed. "You want me to scroll back a full 24 hours?"

"Let's start with the footage from last night's closing."

"Easy enough."

The screen changed again. The Grand Gala was empty. A single guard walked past and disappeared through the north entrance.

"How many people are here overnight?"

"Three guards plus a contract janitorial crew that's here from 11 to 2. Supposed to be the most boring graveyard shift in town."

"No one's ever tried to break in?"

"And hurt the *precious art*?"

Cole smiled at the guard's mock effrontery. "Nice to meet the only other person in New Florence who doesn't give two shits about this stuff."

"Tell me about it. I'm only here because my wife's job relocated. Never date a girl from New Florence. Our first date, she wants me to take her to a paint and sip. So that happened. I sipped, she painted. Jesus."

"Pause it!"

Cole stood up and leaned closer to the first monitor. A shadow tantalized the camera, sweeping across the lens like some tattered black cloak. The officer went back five seconds, then ten. Darkness flashed again and Cole ordered another pause. The camera was blacked out. He stood up straight and rubbed his chin.

"What is it? Want me to go back further?"

The officer's obvious confusion made Cole question him. "You don't see something obstructing the lens?"

"I see the gallery floor."

His tone asked, *What are you smoking?*

Cole knew what he saw. The first screen was dark except for a fringe of light in the lower left corner that proved something was blocking the view.

"Can I see the second camera's footage at this time stamp?"

"Sure."

Cole's throat tightened as he waited. His calves cramped. The second monitor switched from Dimwitter to last night's calm emptiness. The security guard crossed the floor again and headed north.

A man crept into view from the right. Crept wasn't the right word. Slinked, flowed, seeped. Darkness trailed behind him, a spreading shadow. The man was lean and tall, like some rubber doll stretched and mangled past all recovery. He was naked, his cyanotic skin taut against what seemed to be a hundred ribs. His face remained hidden as

55

he placed his hands against *The Lament*. His spine contorted, arms stretching, fingers groping and sweeping across the huge canvas. Then he raked sharp fingernails across his body, slicing the skin all over. He soaked his hands in flows of black blood and smeared it across the painting, making a bleak swirling palimpsest. *The Lament* blackened like something burned and the strange ritual became frantic. The man kept cutting himself, urging the blood forth. He began throwing himself against the painting in great leaps, holding himself suspended in the air like some living paint roller. Then, when no trace of the original painting remained and his own flesh was glistening black, he sank into *The Lament's* wet darkness, a chameleon plunge so abrupt it was as if he'd fallen through the frame and vanished.

Squinting, Cole leaned toward the monitor. As he did, the figure exploded forward, straight at the camera, straight at him, and hung suspended in the air grinning into the lens. Red eyes, red lips. Toothy rictus smile that made the petal-shaped tumors at the corner of his mouth flutter and sway. The figure held this pose and just grinned into the future, seeking this moment, those eyes brighter and hungrier by the second, the face streaked blue and black like war paint, the tongue a searching dark ribbon. Cole got out of the chair, stumbling backwards, digging for the metal and gripping for all his worth until last night's cuts threatened to bleed anew.

"Turn it off!" Cole shouted.

"What in the hell is wrong with—"

"Turn the fucking thing off!"

"I don't understand what's going on, but you're freaking me out. You act like you've seen a ghost. There wasn't jack from either camera."

Cole was quick to nod. Anything to get away from the room. "Right. You're right, you're right. Guess I'm edgy. Going to go see Jampier."

"Need help out?"

"No. I'm good."

"Sure?"

"I could just use some of the *sip* you were talking about. Rough night, you know?"

The officer laughed and clapped Cole on the shoulder, tension easing, though perhaps he was just glad to be rid of the weirdo. Cole didn't need Mikey's *extra* to know.

Cole left and went to the first bathroom he could find. Its stillness and quiet had him spooked but he needed a moment's privacy. He locked the door and stood with his back to the wall texting Mikey, glancing toward the door every half minute. Expecting the handle to jiggle. Hallucinating the shadow of feet at the sill.

Can you come over here?

He responded in moments.

Does this mean I'm hired? followed by *Yes, just let me clean up*.

Cole let out a long breath. His screen went dark from inactivity and he saw his reflected face blue and hideous. Red lips, red eyes. He shrieked and dropped the phone as he flinched against the wall. The bathroom mirror was to his right and he risked a glance. The face Mikey so often called *cute* seemed older and haggard. But human. Normal. He bent to pick up the phone. As he did, it buzzed and he damned near dropped it again.

Dimwitter's name showed on the screen.

"This is Sharpe."

"Where are you?" Jampier's voice. "Security called down to tell me you left in an agitated—"

"I'm still on the administration level. In a bathroom."

"Are you okay?"

"I'm fine. Just a little stomach issue. Are you still in the Grand Gala?"

"Yes."

"I'll be down in a moment."

He pocketed the phone and headed for the door. A noise at his back made him pause. Cole felt a sudden sureness he wasn't alone in the room. If he turned now, he'd see the face from his dream, the face from the camera footage. Grinning at him. Those red eyes, those red lips. He heard a footstep. Knew he did. A presence loomed over his back, vulturing over him. Cole closed his eyes, swallowing, his throat dry. He gripped the metal again, but it was becoming like a sponge with nothing left to squeeze out. The very thought of this sorrowed him. He needed to turn around on his own. Confront the shadow. There was no incantation, no charm for the mind's fear greater than turning around and dispelling what wasn't there. But it *was* there. It would be there. Red eyes, red lips. Hunger. Cold cruelty. Cole shivered. He eased his right hand out of his coat pocket and looked at it. The palm scabbed and injured by the most precious protection he possessed.

If I don't speak now, it will win, he thought. More so if there's nothing there at all. If I don't turn around and look, then what's not there will become real and stay real. I'll have birthed it into the world.

He heard something. It could have been a trickle of water from the tap, some whisper from the HVAC system. But he heard it as a word in his ear.

"Masterpiece."

Cole bit back a scream, got the door open just a crack and crammed his body through in a mad dash down the hall, blind to all signs and directions. He kept close to the wall like a blind man stripped of cane or service dog. He'd taken the elevator up, but he wasn't about to trap himself inside it now.

The showcase marble steps that led between gallery levels weren't in evidence here. No doubt to conceal the very concept of administrative offices. He pushed through a gray door into a cold stairwell and went down a floor before reemerging in the world of art. Cole found himself hurrying past displays of Native American artifacts. Totems and shamanistic images under glass. What he'd give to have one of those long-dead holy men at his side now, protecting his flight with forgotten magic.

He found the marble steps and descended. The further down he went, the more people he encountered. Sounds of chatting, sounds of murmurs. A lot more people now, to his heart's gladness. At the landing between the 2nd floor and the lobby, Cole stopped to recover himself, wiping the sweat off his forehead with the sleeve of his coat. Gaining control of his breathing was the hardest task. He stood there like an exhausted marathon runner. Lungs don't sip air when the pulse demands crude gulps.

He texted Mikey again.

How far away are you?

Mikey's response was almost immediate.

Half an hour. Just now getting a ride.

Getting a ride, Cole thought, knowing Mikey didn't mean calling a cab or using an app. He was sneaking the idea into someone's head. *Hey, how about you give me a ride downtown? Sounds like a great idea, right?*

No time to fret over a telepath's morals.

Cole pocketed the phone, becoming sensitive to the number of people coming and going on the stairs, flashing annoyance at the fool loitering in the middle of the landing. He took a deeper, more controlled breath and committed himself to the final flight of steps. The trembling in his legs surprised him. His calves were unsteady. Must have been his body's way of shaking off adrenaline and fear, the way a dog wrings water off its back.

His gait wasn't much better as he entered the Grand Gala. Jampier stood alone in front of Dimwitter, engaged in another mock conversation. He broke it off as soon as Cole arrived and said, "What's the end game here? Is there any plan at all?"

Impatience colored his tone as it hadn't before. Perhaps the notion of standing here holding pretend discussions had wearied him.

"Like I said, based on past evidence, the trance will

59

change at some point. He'll walk out of here. My guess is tonight."

"Where will he go? Home?"

"I'm not sure. I lost the woman I was tailing last night. I won't make the same mistake this time."

"I'll have the security guards follow him too."

"That's not advisable."

Jampier scoffed. "Mr. Sharpe, you may not understand how this situation has escalated. Mr. Dimwitter is the *head* of the Directorate. The city's most knowledgeable and experienced curator. A man of *international* reputation—"

"I'm sure he's a hell of a guy."

"President of the AAMD."

"Sounds medical."

Jampier's eyes narrowed. "The Association of Art Museum Directors. Mr. Dimwitter in short *is* the most important man in New Florence. I won't turn his safety over to someone whose state of mind appears to be—"

"What? What's my state of mind?"

"*Questionable.*"

Cole nodded. Who was he to argue against an obvious point?

"Do what you need to do. Mr. Dimwitter contacted me because he wanted the situation kept on the downlow as much as possible. That was his judgment call. But by all means, go against his wishes and bring in the cops."

"I didn't say anything about the police," Jampier whispered. "I just want our own people around for whatever happens. The Directorate takes care of its own."

You mean the Directorate covers its own ass, Cole thought, and went outside to wait for Mikey.

Mikey arrived true to his word thirty minutes later, and Cole recognized the car and the driver. His neighbor across the hall, Brad, was grinning as he completed his chauffeur duties. Mikey got out, gave the roof of the car two happy little slaps, wished Brad a good day, and shut the door. As Mikey stepped away, Cole noticed Brad's expression change to cloudy confusion.

"Hey, handsome, your business partner is here," he said, all smiles for a second. That soon changed and he glanced over his shoulder at Brad's departing car. "Is there a problem, Detective?"

"Maybe I just need to get used to how you operate. If we're going to be spending a lot of time together on a *professional* basis."

Mikey shrugged. "I may be a fallen woman, but I'm sure your pure cowboy ways can redeem me. The redemption can wait though, right? Because I didn't come all this way for a scolding, and it's hypocritical since you only called me down here to try and get a sense of Dimwitter's mind."

Cole flushed. "You're right. I'm—"

"Apologize later. Let's get to work."

Cole motioned him toward the gallery doors. "I'll tell you what's happened."

"I can fill myself in much faster."

"I think I'd rather tell you."

"*Cole.*"

They looked at each other.

"I'm on your side," Mikey said. "Always and forever. Scouts honor."

Cole glanced down at his feet and nodded. Of course, Mikey was right. He stood still and let Mikey come up to him. He looked at Cole's forehead, eyes shifting from left to right like he was reading a screen.

"*Fuck!*" Mikey sprang back. "Oh shit, that's about the scariest thing I've ever seen. That face. Just grinning into the camera like that. Nightmare fuel. And then the bathroom stuff."

"I'm embarrassed by it."

"You shouldn't be."

"I scared myself like a damn kid afraid of a campfire ghost in the middle of the morning."

"That wasn't a campfire ghost. Fangsy was there."

Cole fought off a shiver. "Come on, Mikey, you can't know that. I don't have eyes in the back of my head you could see from."

"It's the level of your terror. People only have so much innate fear even when they're amped up. It's like body temperature. Some people can run a little hot, others a little cold. When it comes to fear, you run on the low side. There was something standing behind holding a torch to your fear thermometer, and you responded to it."

Hearing this, imagining he'd made the narrowest of escapes, Cole shoved his hands into his pockets. Gripped the metal.

He saw Mikey's gaze drop down in notice.

"You know something, handsome? There's one single thing about you I can't read at all. It's what you have in there. What you keep touching. It never has the same shape in your thoughts. I'd say it has no shape at all. It's like you've got a cloud in your pocket. I won't lie, I even thought about sneaking a peek while you were dreaming the other night."

"Why didn't you?"

"Maybe you're special enough I wanted to earn a little show and tell from you."

Cole felt his heartbeat going fast. Mikey's eyes were wide and more innocent than they had any right to be, yet the innocence was as genuine as anything Cole ever saw. The look of some fairy tale maiden on the verge of receiving the prince's kiss. He deserves to see the metal, Cole thought, certain the idea was his own. The unexpected giddiness, too. As he began pulling his right hand free still gripping the metal, Cole felt like a man about to drop to one knee and proffer a wedding ring.

Dimwitter came out the door with Jampier and three security guards following. Jampier saw Cole and gave a frantic wave. He and Mikey rushed to him as Dimwitter kept going, his pace a little faster than Susan Wills's as he headed down the street.

"He just turned around while I was talking," Jampier said. "I thought you said he wouldn't move until night!"

"I based that on the last person."

"Well, follow if you're going to follow. We're not losing him."

Jampier and the guards moved on. Cole looked at Mikey. It wasn't even noon.

"Think it means anything that he didn't wait until dark?"

"It's always dusk in Midnight Village."

They set out, following Jampier and his men who kept about twenty yards behind Dimwitter. They passed facades covered in exquisite graffiti, as New Florence dedicated blocks upon blocks to urban art. Dimwitter detoured into alleyways, brick walls covered with cartoon menageries on both sides. He led them down sidewalks flowing in fanciful chalk drawings far removed from last night's sinister weave of images. They passed street art vendors hawking watercolor postcards and originals of their own making, even the worst showing obvious competency and skill. A mother and her daughter sat on a bench, posing for a man who developed their image on his canvas like a gradual Polaroid of oil paints. They were moving among the deepest and richest veins of the city's artistic commitments now, where it could be said New Florence was no city with an art walk but rather an art walk doubling as a city from its core to its fringes, and if every door in every house were flung open you would glimpse within framed Picassos and Van Goghs and Rembrandts, except the names were Smith and Adams and Richardson, the work of common people taught and tutored from birth in this kingdom of art, each capable of dashing off masterpieces to decorate the walls.

Dimwitter's course was taking them behind the Crayon Box, a southern trajectory where the city's high-minded notions were less in evidence and easier to disprove. The streets became dirtier, the buildings blander and shorter, hidden like despised children forced to crouch out of sight behind their taller, nobler siblings in a family portrait. Unseen didn't mean absent. In the years after his father's death, Cole used to ramble through this part of the city in search of a kindred ugliness, a twinship darkness whatever the form. Something that echoed the dejection and rejection within him that despised all art. In hindsight he wondered if these streets and passages behind the Crayon Box's waterfall of color had given him his first inkling of Midnight Village's existence long before he met Mikey. There'd been a sense of another city, a dark double that also refused him, and the ache of that refusal kept him coming back to revel in the pain.

Mikey touched Cole's hand and pulled him back. They dropped to a slower pace, letting a gap spread between themselves and Jampier.

"There's a portal less than a quarter mile ahead. Dimwitter's heading straight for it."

Cole stepped to the left and peered down the sidewalk. He saw the shimmer.

"If he goes through, will Jampier and his men be able to follow?"

"I really don't know."

"What happens if they do get into Midnight Village?"

"You know the answer."

Cole grimaced. "Can you keep all of us safe?"

"It's a passport, not an umbrella. There's something else. I've been trying to pick up on Dimwitter's thoughts. Not having a lot of luck. Dude's not attractive at all."

"It's fine if you can't."

"No, it's not fine at all. Because I've picked up some snippets. I thought you said he's catatonic."

"Like the woman from last night."

Mikey shook his head. "I don't think he's out of it at all. More like he's trying hard to act like it."

Cole halted and tried to comprehend the implications. He didn't have the luxury of a lengthy consideration. Dimwitter passed through the shimmer. All signs pointed to Jampier and his men following. He called Jampier's name, telling him to stop. They ignored him and passed through the portal too.

"Come on," Cole said, and he and Mikey dashed after them.

All color became muted and the sky prevailed in dusk light. Jampier and his men were rooted in place by confusion as Dimwitter kept moving.

"What the hell is this?" Jampier said. "What happened to the sky? It was just morning."

Cole moved in front of them, holding up his hands to quiet them. The fourteen wraiths were already circling.

"You have to turn back. My friend might be able to get you out of here."

"We don't go anywhere without Mr. Dimwitter."

Jampier moved ahead. His security guards were less certain.

The wraiths made their silent drops. Three in front of Jampier. Eleven around the security guards. Mikey grabbed Cole by the coat and pulled him clear of the attack. The wraiths' flailing arms stretched to envelop the others. Jampier made a gargled cry as an inky black garrote ensnared his neck. His eyes bulged and his face went crimson in an instant, a striking reminder of blood's power to paint faster than the quickest brush.

Cole looked between the dying men, overwhelmed by helplessness. He turned to Mikey and said, "Give Jampier my passport."

"*What?*"

"Do it! Hurry. Save them one at a time and get them out of here. I'll go after Dimwitter."

"The wraiths—"

"You can come rescue me. It's what you're best at."

He heard Mikey shouting behind him as he turned and

fled down the empty sidewalk. His calves were shaking again, and his stomach felt hollow. He saw Dimwitter up ahead reducing speed as Cole closed on him. Dimwitter was about to turn a corner and, for just a second, he seemed to check to see if Cole was following. A sly look. A mistake. Without Mikey's warning, Cole might have missed it.

Cole stopped. Dimwitter must have realized whatever ruse he'd orchestrated had failed. He stopped too, turned to Cole, smiled and bowed.

"What the hell is this?"

"Follow me, Mr. Sharpe. There's something you'll want to see."

"I'm not interested in anything you have to show me."

"Even your father's soul?"

This answer was so unexpected and loathsome Cole almost charged the man. But he kept his place.

"You've heard that art immortalizes, Mr. Sharpe. Here it eternalizes under the skill of a true master."

Cole heard footsteps at his back. Mikey was running toward him, shouting. The wraiths were overhead.

"No, not him! Sorry! Go eat elsewhere!"

Mikey reached Cole, panting in his breathlessness. Cole clung to him with his left arm. The wraiths swept out of sight.

"Don't let the invitation become a command, Mr. Sharpe. The invitation's yoke is easy. The command carries the burden of many sacrifices. Come along. See your father. Understand his fate."

"My father's dead! That's his fate."

Cole wiped his eyes.

"Come see him and so many others look out at you through vivid flames."

A force tried to pull him backward. It was Mikey's arm pressed across his stomach.

Dimwitter laughed.

"Come on, Cole," Mikey said, and Cole began to

surrender. He walked backwards several yards as Dimwitter's laughter continued.

"You'll marvel at how your father's eyes blink at you."

"My father's dead!" Cole shouted again and stood in a daze as Dimwitter's laughter ceased.

"Is the invitation refused?"

When Cole didn't answer, Mikey stepped between them and raised both middle fingers. "Here's an artist statement for you: go fuck yourself."

Then he led Cole out of Midnight Village.

They sat in Cole's apartment through the evening hours, with Cole speaking very little. Part of him wished he'd just taken Dimwitter's offer, not out of fear of repercussions but because he felt whatever he would have seen couldn't be worse than what his imagination had already conjured. He couldn't escape his father's face. But his father was dead. Everyone who got trapped in the *Gone By Morning* exhibit was dead.

Except him.

Mikey brought him coffee.

"I might be able to do something," he said. "Take the images out of your mind."

"Maybe I need them."

"You don't. I can see—"

"Quit looking."

Mikey backed off. Cole thought he was going to leave, but he went to the bathroom. The shower started. Cole considered stripping his clothes and getting under the water with him. But he stayed put, staring at the black TV screen, taking in the details of his living room like he was a stranger. His might be the only coffee table in New Florence without a showy, oversized art book. Maybe his aversion to art was shortsighted, he thought. Holding him back in this case. As his thoughts began to refocus on the case, he found the terrible images of his father dwindling. This was incentive enough to keep his mind on its new course.

When Mikey came back, he was just in a towel, his shaggy brown hair darkened by dampness. Cole admired his lean torso and said, "I've been thinking I should know more about art. You've just given me another reason. I'm sure someone like Dimwitter could compare you to 100 paintings or statues right now."

"I wouldn't want someone *like Dimwitter* anywhere near me."

"I guess all I've got is David. That's Michelangelo, right? Image of male perfection."

"David's got the better build. But I," Mikey said, letting the towel fall, "am far better hung."

Cole laughed at that, but his mirth was brief. Watching Mikey retrieve the towel, he said, "I'm trying to understand what Fangsy wants. Whatever else he is, he's an artist. It doesn't matter where in the world you go, they want the same thing. Call it respect or prestige or recognition. Call it sympathy, understanding, a shared wavelength."

"I'd say that's right."

"All those things are synonyms for *audience*. And every artist wants the audience to come to *them*."

"What does that mean?"

"I think I'm his audience. Maybe I always was. Maybe that's why I survived the fire."

"There were a lot of people trapped by the glass, not just you."

"Sure, they were there. But people can be present and not be the audience. The artist decides that, using whatever criteria they choose. All those deaths, just for me."

Mikey came and knelt beside him, his hands on Cole's left forearm. "Why don't we leave? Get the hell out of New Florence and start something in another state. Or halfway around the world for that matter. I can make it happen. If the way I go about it bothers you, we can always make amends later."

"I'm not sure it would matter." There was too much truth in the statement and Cole saw the downcast look in Mikey's eyes. It made him lean forward and shout, "Fangsy, you can go to hell! I won't come to you! You want me as an audience, you can come crawling!"

"Jesus," Mikey said with nervous laughter.

Cole got up and took Mikey to the bedroom.

They slept together that night, protecting each other from intimations of Fangsy that never came. Cole heard no strange noises, saw no disturbing shadows. Even when he had to go to the bathroom in the middle of the night and face his inevitable reflection in the vanity, Fangsy was not leering back. When he returned, seeking Mikey's warmth, he fought a sudden certainty that Mikey would somehow be replaced with Fangsy's long, cobalt leanness, undiscovered until he'd already snuggled up against the cold flesh. But Mikey's heat dispelled that terror and he fell back into a sound sleep uninterrupted until his phone buzzed at 8AM.

Dimwitter.

Cole considered the screen a moment. He answered but did not speak.

"The invitation's revoked. The command is given, and the sacrifices will be great."

Mikey made the faintest stirring. His face looked relaxed and untroubled.

"I don't answer to your commands."

"It is not my command, Cole. I'm but the messenger."

"Where are you calling from?"

"West Gallery."

"Am I supposed to come over?"

"Not at all. Go to any gallery you like. Each offers the same burning example."

Cole's sudden distress must have burst across Mikey's

mind too, because he woke with a start, on the verge of hyperventilating.

"Dimwitter!" Cole shouted. But the call was over and he contemplated the silence with growing dread before going to the bathroom to splash cold water on his face. Mikey stood behind him, hurrying into his clothes.

"He said go to any gallery?"

"That's right."

"Which one are we going to? Or should we split up?"

"I really want you to stay here."

"I'm with you every step from now on."

Cole bunched his fists and then willed his fingers open as he took a purposeful exhale. The dream was alive in his mind again. As he turned to the bathroom door, he found he was walking through flames in a building of glass. He couldn't even see Mikey despite hearing his voice and he stopped in what he knew must be his apartment hallway. He closed his eyes and willed the dream away. When he looked again, he only saw Mikey, looking pensive.

"Did anxiety bring it on?"

"No. Certainty did. I think I know what the plan must be. Dimwitter said I'd find a burning example. Today is Free Day. The schools will be out in force. All of them. Tons of field trips. Maybe thousands of kids."

Realization seemed to dawn in Mikey's expression. He either pieced it out for himself or just saw what Cole was imagining.

"Not just one gallery fire but dozens. Twenty or thirty sequels to *Gone By Morning* all featuring hundreds of kids."

"I'm going to the West Gallery to confront Dimwitter. He's been doing Fangsy's bidding from the beginning, but I don't think he's a fraud. He's got ambition but he cares about art. Values a painting above human life. I can't believe he'd be willing to see so much of it burn. There's got to be something else in it for him."

But Cole couldn't fathom what it was.

—◣◥—

They joined a big throng filing their way inside the West Gallery. The school children were present in horrific abundance and empty buses lined the streets. Most were elementary school age but here and there groups of teens looked at their phones and giggled. The high-pitched banter of boys and girls sounded as ominous to Cole as any song composed by the musicians of Midnight Village. It seemed a foreshadowing of screams and the white condensation of their excited breaths reminded him of smoke.

The ticket desks were vacant, but a much larger supplementary staff were on hand, all dressed in black slacks and jackets, navy blue shirts and lace-up Oxfords polished to a gleam. He studied their expressions.

"Think they're any good in a fight?" Mikey said.

"What?"

"Museum ushers."

"Are you looking to take one on?"

"If Dimwitter's a traitor, they might be in on it too."

"I was just thinking that."

Mikey smiled. "I didn't have to read your mind to know."

The ushers went on smiling and directing groups, offering adults and older students maps and little information sheets, instructions for accessing QR-coded guided tours and the enhanced experience offered by the Directorate's free app. He detected nothing but joy and earnestness in their behavior, but he asked Mikey for verification.

"The ones I can read aren't conspiring on anything," he said. "Though I'd tell the teachers to keep the boys from getting too chummy with the bald dude on the right."

Cole frowned. As soon as they gained admittance, he pressed ahead, studying the entrances and exits, imagining foot traffic patterns if each room burst into simultaneous flames. White sprinkler head cover plates dotted the ceiling. He could only assume they were operative, but would water extinguish the sort of hellfire that had killed his father?

"It's going to be different this time," Mikey said, and Cole realized he was verbalizing the very thought he had in his head.

"It's got to be. Let's separate a bit. See if we can spot Dimwitter."

"You sure?"

"Positive. Text if you find him."

Mikey made his way out of the room. Cole stood there a minute longer, listening to the sound of the children, picking out individual voices, the dumb jokes they made, the teasing and taunts they threw at each other. Here and there annoyed teachers tried to explain the importance of a painting, trying to get them to *look*. A wasted effort on most, but Cole found exceptions, kids really into it all, silent and contemplative, captivated.

He walked over to a painting that was just fine gradations of different shades of yellow awaiting contemplation. Cole gave the room another cursory search for Dimwitter and then gave his full attention to the framed piece in front of him.

Ok, art, he thought. Enlighten me.

For the first few moments he felt only pointlessness. The colors didn't arrange themselves into an epiphany, not even an arrow pointing him in the right direction. But as Cole stared, he sensed a presence sidling up to him, like a massive block of ice just beyond his peripheral vision. An intelligence versed in art and ready to teach its truths in brutal lessons.

Masterpiece.

"You're not killing anyone else like you did my dad."

A banshee's wail sounded through Cole's mind, driving away his bravado. A force spun him around and propelled him forward. He stumbled and flailed through the crowds, drawing rebukes from teachers and chaperones. Cole struggled to keep his wits, trying to call out for Mikey's help, but there seemed to be a muzzle on his thoughts. His head became a quiet place, and as he went room to room, he noticed the children were hushing. The art lectures became more pronounced, more authoritative.

"Notice how Du Paurier's model seems to be staring right at you—"

"And this is called surrealism because the representation is—"

"Painters from this time period were called Modernists because—"

Cole bent forward like he was being led by the nose. The voices he could still hear all seemed to be slowing, every vowel becoming nonsense elongations.

He stumbled into the Founder's Room. He had it to himself. The emptiness felt unnatural, pre-arranged. Cole faced the portrait of Payne Alhuile: dark hair, kind eyes, lips that smiled at progeny.

Talentless fool and apostate. The final sacrifice.

He was yanked to his left to confront the self-portrait of Thomas DiLeppo. White hair, gray eyes, a somewhat bored expression.

An artist cannot create good work when he loathes his model. The fifth sacrifice.

Cole was jerked a few feet to his right, squared front and center before the self-portrait of Armus Constantine. Blood red hair and beard, pale face, tight lips.

Competent with nature scenes, so I honored him in a forest no longer extant. The first sacrifice.

Cole was spun like a top, so that he pirouetted to the next painting.

Timothy Andreeson. Flamboyant in a blue suit, the brim of a yellow derby hat cocked high above his right eye like a sunrise happening over his shoulder.

STOLEN PALLOR

Steely determination clothed in girlish satins. Hardest of all to kill. I mixed his blood into my paints.

The process continued, taking Cole back and forth across the room, a confrontation of fourteen paintings, a condemnation of fourteen names.

Until only Royland G. Bivvens remained. Cole stared and recognized and understood. Traces of this portrait's features remained in the face that had stared at him through the security camera. Cole detected new traits unnoticed when he stood before the painting with Susan Wills. Hunger. Anger. Condescension. The suggestion of the skull emerging through the skin. A little mole at both corners of the mouth. So many secret confessions kept in the sunken eyes.

A Bruegel toiling among Constables. A Goya at war with a handful of Copleys. A Munch and Ensor before Munch and Ensor ever drew breath. Weak visions cannot grow an artist's colony. I created my own.

"Midnight Village," Cole said, though he thought he was only mouthing the words.

The start of my long masterpiece.

"Killing people isn't art. It's butchery. You murdered my father and all of those people."

Gone By Morning *gave them eternity. True art is not the hour of a passing fad. Attend now to the latest crop of immortals.*

Shouts came from several rooms and Cole found himself freed. He ran into the next gallery and found groups of children standing before various paintings like they were beholding the light of God. Parents and teachers went from child to child, waving hands in front of their faces, even shaking some of them by the shoulders.

"What's wrong with you, Matt?"

"Stop this game right now!"

"We're going back to school if you don't start behaving this instant."

Cole heard variations on the theme as he skirted the

edges of the crowds, moving from one gallery to another. Seven elementary school children stood fixated before a painting of ballerinas by Degas. A dozen high school kids crowded around a bouquet of flowers painted by Maria van Oosterwyck with the enthusiasm of boys from a more innocent generation experiencing their first peep show. In another room, an entire class of middle school students, some thirty children, were looking at different paintings, possessed by the same overmastering attentiveness.

My God, he thought. If there's a fire they won't even move. They'll just burn in place.

All he could think about was a gallery fire from his childhood and how the drape over the building and the painting dropped at the same time. How the sunlight stormed down on them in what should have been a burst of illumination meant to glorify the art.

He thought of every story and legend he knew about vampires burning in the sunlight. Could the same hold true of their blood? If *The Lament* could be taken from its place in the Grand Gala and hauled outside, would it burst into flame . . . the way *Gone By Morning* had?

But none of the paintings in this or any gallery would ever be exposed to sunlight. The only windows were in the lobby. So how would the fire start? Arson? Rigged explosives? The methods seemed too crude, too—*inartistic*.

He started to text Mikey when his phone received one from Dimwitter.

The masterpiece will be finished tonight.

There were several video attachments from multiple galleries. Hundreds of mesmerized children ignoring frustrated chaperones, turning in unison, and marching out the door.

The children around Cole now began to move too.

"Wait? Where are you going?"

"Amanda? Steven?"

"Come back here right now!"

Cole texted Mikey.

Where are you? I'm in the third gallery.

A moment later his phone buzzed again. Another text from Dimwitter.

You did not accept the Master's generous invitation. Know the sacrifices to come are all upon your head.

More videos followed. Children streaming from the galleries, moving into the streets, heading out en masse. Who could calculate how many students all together? Several hundred? More than a thousand? The police and the teachers might secure a small fraction, but most would follow the children to an unwitting doom. Cole knew where they must be going, and how wrong his assumption had been. Fangsy the artist had already done a gallery fire. Fangsy the artist did *not* repeat himself. The children would come to him just as Susan Wills and those before her had answered the summons. To be an audience? To serve in some other way? Cole's careering imagination couldn't keep up with the possible horrors.

He moved through the rooms, finding the same situation every time. But one sight was worst of all. One sight terrified and worried him above all others.

Mikey stood still in front of a painting about three feet long and wide. Three children stood next to him. He was the only adult who shared their affliction and Cole rushed to him, shaking him. "Mikey, please. Can you hear me? Blink or something if you can hear me!"

Mikey remained statue still.

Cole spun away from him, took out his phone and texted Dimwitter.

Stop this. Whatever you want, whatever Fangsy wants, I'll come to Midnight Village. I'll give myself up.

The response came back at once:

No.

Cole cursed, put away the phone and pivoted back to Mikey. He leaned in and kissed him, pressing his lips to Mikey's with all the passion and devotion he could muster.

When he pulled back, all his hopes hinged upon a fairy tale awakening that just couldn't be wrung from the grim reality of the moment. He stepped back, shaking his head, looking at the captive children and the children now turning to leave. The teachers and chaperones stood dumbfounded and lost.

Cole turned to glare at the painting that had captured Mikey. An idea came to mind. Desperate, last ditch. Hail Mary.

He reached into his coat pocket, gripped the metal and thought, Dad, give me the strength to do this.

Cole grabbed the painting by the frame and tore it from its mounting hooks. Turning, he held it aloft and shouted, "Listen to me. There's only one way to save the kids. There's something wrong with the paintings. They have to burn!"

The dozen or so adults in the room turned from the students to gape at him, standing there with the painting and the truth held aloft like one tablet of the Ten Commandments, suffused in teeth gnashing righteousness, enrobed with the light of salvation.

"I can prove it! See what happens when sunlight hits the painting."

A woman in her forties stepped forward. "What the hell is all this, some sort of performance art? Children, if this is all part of some act, you better—"

Cole smashed the frame down hard against the floor. He felt he was crashing a chair over someone's head. The joints broke open in the right corner and he leveraged the toe of his foot against the crack and jerked upward until the bottom of the frame splintered and fell apart.

A gasp came from the adults, for they were all true residents of New Florence. He saw right away that even in the depths of this crisis his solution profaned their beliefs. They needed to be shown the absolute reality.

He took the painting and charged forward with it even as hands grabbed at him from all sides. Cole swore and shouted at the fools, determined to reach the lobby with its high east-facing windows. He'd not surrender the painting until he plunged the canvas into the lobby's generous sunlight and witnessed it become ash in his hands.

But he was moving against the density of children and the adults who saw him as an immediate threat, a crazier man in a crazy situation. Hands battered him, arms wrapped around his waist and legs. Cole soldiered through. His body felt like the damaged frame, straining at every seam and sinew, bones threatening to snap. The sunlight gleamed ahead of him as he neared the lobby. Another push. One more push. One final effort. For the children.

For Mikey.

Dad, just this one bit of help. Just this one.

He was driven to his knees by a tackle. He kept crawling, pushing the painting just ahead of him. The transition strip between the room's checkerboard tile and the lobby's carpet took on all the urgency of a marathon finish line. Someone kicked him in the ribs. He rolled over but clung to the painting and thrashed forward. The canvas bumped over the transition strip and eased into the sunlight.

Fire sprang up in the spot and burned with the purity of candle fire. "See!" Cole cried, but he had almost no air, no voice. The fire would speak loud enough. He pushed further and the fire spread. He looked to the adults standing over him, desperate for their realization. He found himself confronted by the gallery staff. Behind them the children were walking out the door. Cole held the burning canvas up to them and said, "See? Gone by morning. Destroy the paintings. Make them burn."

"This is madness," one said.

Another was on the phone. To the police. To Dimwitter. To someone.

"Yes, sir," he said. "Yes, a lunatic. Schizophrenic by the looks. Maybe a psychotic break triggered by the chaos."

"Poor man," said a woman, armed with a fire extinguisher.

Behind them, glimpsed through their legs, the children slipped away. There was another figure, taller than the rest, taking the same affectless walk.

Mikey.

Cole reached out through the space between them and held one trembling hand out until Mikey was out the door and out of sight.

I love you.

Cole spent the next several hours bound hand and foot and slumped in a corner of a storage room containing marble busts and primitive masks. He wept and fretted for an audience of empty, vacant-eyed faces. Nothing but his phone and keys had been confiscated and he'd not been stripped. Unconsciousness would have been a blessing, the gift of not having to imagine what was happening across New Florence or the fate of the students.

Or of—

He squeezed his eyes shut tight against dark imaginings and started composing a letter to Mikey in his thoughts. A love letter, a confession, a rambling explanation of who he was, what he felt. Maybe Mikey knew these things, having digested all the years of Cole's life in a few minutes. There was still no harm in formalizing and organizing it. Offering it. He wrote and rewrote and scratched out and inserted against the chaos of indistinct paper with an indistinct pen, nurturing a fond hope that somehow Mikey was out there registering it all and smiling. Smiling and not dead.

It all comes down to this: I was lost and maybe I'm still lost because I'm a goddamn romantic, but my dad was romantic too; my mom swore this up and down, romantic despite all the practicality and the logic and the reasoning. I like myself for being romantic and having imagination and just wanting everything to work out no matter how depressed I got or how bleak. A non-romantic would look at you or look at me and say nothing between us could ever work or make sense but I think a romantic is forever innocent and innocent people can be in love because when you're not complicated there are only simple pleasures or the pleasures of simplicity and I Love You isn't a complicated sentence to diagram.

He went on like this, falling into a delirium that didn't break until the sound of footsteps echoed from the hallway. Cole wriggled himself into a better sitting position and mustered bravado in the face of his total defeat.

The door opened and Dimwitter entered.

"Mr. Sharpe," he said. "I'd imagine you're ready for a change in scenery."

He was dressed in a full tuxedo just like the members of the Directorate had worn when they perished in the fire. The desiccated remains of a rose was pinned to the lapel. Dimwitter must have noticed Cole's fixation, because he gave the dead flower a sniff and then made a preening rotation with his arms held out. "I've kept myself in good shape, haven't I? The Directorate purchased these for all of its members just for the *Gone By Morning* exhibit. I did in fact wear it that day—as I stood in the living room where my easel and canvas were ready. I turned on the TV. The news was covering the event live, of course. I still remember how the black curtain draped over all that glass billowed a little at the edges. It was not a heavy cloth, though it may have seemed that way to you, since you were under it."

"Why did you sell everyone out to Fangsy? What was in it for you?"

"It was not an easy choice. Great art often requires dark compromises. My master made that morning the first day of my instruction. I was to stand before the TV and paint picture after picture, as fast as I could. How I sped, treating each canvas more like a series of Post-It Notes. First, the glass covered in black cloth. Then the glass revealed and lit from within by brilliant fire. The third canvas—nothing but anguished faces. I painted death and reaction to death. The work was so crude. Even then I thought I could do better if I just had a few moments to slow down, to decide, to correct. But I was not allowed. In the hour between the curtain's drop and the deaths of two hundred people, your father among them, I produced ten watercolors. My fingers, my wrist, my forearm developed an arthritic ache that kept me from going on. I thought about that pain and how *art* is the beginning of arthritis. One of art's ancient root words means to fit things together. Art is about joints. I knew then my mind was opening to the suffering my teacher said existed at the center of true art. Pain joins the audience and the artist through the work, and in that joining something new and terrible enters the world."

"You make it sound like a birth."

"Yes."

"Congrats on letting Fangsy fuck you."

Anger flashed through Dimwitter's expression, followed by a sort of pity. He squatted and began to undo Cole's knots.

"We're all children of art and therefore children of artists. Tonight, in Midnight Village, you will see how well the children have repaid their father."

He went on relaxing the ropes. Cole's muscles were sore and stiff, but he had a size and strength advantage. Dimwitter seemed not to realize, even as he helped pull Cole to his feet. Cole wasted little time lunging at him, punching him in the face and gut. Dimwitter backed up a step but was otherwise unfazed. Then he grabbed Cole by his coat and hoisted him into the air and held him there like a father rejoicing in his newborn.

"Yes," he said. "Children of art must serve their father well. Come and see how the grateful brood of this city have given themselves to the great work at hand."

STOLEN PALLOR

—◢◣◤◥—

New Florence was muted and subdued as they drove to the Central Gallery. The clock on the dash read 9:15. Few people on the streets. Most colors came from flashing police cars. Law enforcement had a big presence across the Crayon Box tonight, which amused Dimwitter enough to elicit a chuckle as they parked in his official spot near the entrance. Both men got out and started walking down the street until the chaotic lights were at their backs.

"They're hunting for the students," he said. "They can't conceive of how they just disappeared, so they've convinced themselves the children must be squirreled away in the skyscrapers somewhere. Now they search from building to building."

They continued on, putting the Crayon Box behind them. Cole knew where Dimwitter was going, a more direct route to the portal than the one he'd taken yesterday.

"How many did Fangsy take?"

"As many as he required."

"Goddamnit, give me a number!"

"500."

Cole whispered the number to himself multiple times and still couldn't make it seem real.

"Again, I remind you this would not be if you'd accepted yesterday's kind invitation. How you must have replayed that scenario countless times in your imagination with a different outcome. Wish fulfillment is its own art."

"They're safe, aren't they? Tell me this is some new kind of art Fangsy is doing. Make the parents worry and call their grief his canvas. But in the end the children come back—"

"I assure you, Mr. Sharpe, the children will not be coming back. They are eternal now."

"Eternal?"

Dimwitter put his arm around Cole like a father about to offer his son warm advice. "Do you know the Judgment of Solomon?"

"Is it a painting?"

"It's many paintings, in fact. One of many stories from the Bible that intrigues the creative mind."

"I know the Bible about as well as I know paintings."

Dimwitter laughed. "Two women come to Solomon, one with a dead baby, the other with a live one. Each claim to be the living child's true mother, and petition Solomon for its custodianship. How is he to decide? What does his vaunted wisdom tell him?"

"I think I do know this story," Cole said.

"Of course. Certain tales permeate through history, don't they? Art indexes that permeation as much as it aids the process. The Judgment of Solomon is the subject of at least fourteen famous paintings. I believe Raphael's was the first. I always preferred Claeissens' rendition, with the dead baby on the floor, a nearby dog sniffing at it as if to determine the viability of the meat. Much superior to Barra's interpretation, so cold and distant, more interested in the architecture of Solomon's palace than the human condition. My Master's favorite is—"

"Is there a point to this art history lesson?"

"I only mean to prepare you for how my Master's wisdom exceeds Solomon's, who ordered the living baby cleaved in two. I told you art is about joints—and joining. Implicit then is that art must also interest itself with disassembling, rearranging, reconstructing. Solomon was no artist. He did not understand all the ways to divvy up the child, all the possible *uses*—"

"Christ," Cole said. "I didn't want to believe you were so far gone. You exchanged blood for paint a long time ago."

"And death for life."

"So there's more than *art lessons* here. Fangsy promised to make you immortal."

83

"Will you never understand, Mr. Sharpe? The only true immortality *is* art."

They were approaching the shimmer. The doorway to Midnight Village was wide open for them. Just as they reached it, a figure stepped out of the adjacent alley. Cole caught sight of a blur in his peripheral vision before a barreling force knocked him to the ground. As he fought off dizziness and struggled to turn over, Cole heard a voice that made him think he was hallucinating. Dimwitter's words flashed through his mind as a warning—*Wish fulfillment is its own art.*

But Mikey standing there grappling with Dimwitter wasn't wish fulfillment. It was real, wonderfully real, and Cole scrambled up to help. When he got to his feet, he realized Mikey needed none. His hands were on Dimwitter's head and Dimwitter was kneeling, spasming, his eyes locked on Mikey's gaze.

Mikey was muttering something indistinct but familiar, words Cole's own lips had traced. Cole didn't dare speak for fear of interrupting Mikey, but he risked moving a few steps closer to listen.

He heard his own boyish voice come from Mikey's mouth.

"Why do I have to be there?"

His father's voice came from Dimwitter's answer. "Because if I suffer, you suffer. It's in the contract."

"What about Mom's death?" Cole said in a low voice, just as the words came from Mikey too. "Was that in the contract, too?"

Cole stepped back. Mikey held Dimwitter in place for another minute. When he let go, Dimwitter fell onto his side and curled into a fetal position, whispering, "Dad . . . the fire . . ."

Mikey stepped back, blinking. He seemed lost for a second. Then he looked at Cole and they locked each other in a fierce embrace.

"I thought you were dead," Cole said, wiping his eyes. "I saw you in the gallery and you were—"

"When I saw the kids getting weird all around me, I tried to tap into whatever they were hearing. It overwhelmed me for a bit. I was lined up with the rest of the students in Midnight Village before I came to my senses."

"You just snapped out of it?"

"*You* snapped me out of it. I was right. I can read your thoughts from miles away. Hell of a letter you wrote me, handsome."

Dimwitter moaned. Cole looked down at him.

"You gave him—*my dream*?"

"I've had an echo of it with me since I started the process of helping you get rid of it. Figured I'd give the bastard a little taste of what you've been through. Right now, he *is* you at that moment. All your fear, all that terror. It'll keep him down long enough to let us get out of here."

"Get out of here? Mikey, we have to get to those kids. You said you were with them. What were they doing?"

"Waiting."

"For what?"

Mikey just stared at him. Cole repeated the question.

"Fangsy has them, Cole. I'm sorry."

"You're *sorry*?"

"What else do you want me to say? There's nothing you can do about it. There's nothing I can do about it. Sometimes evil wins."

"Not this time. Not yet."

"There's only two of us. We're not going to find any allies in Midnight Village. The whole place is a Fangsy fan club."

"One child," Cole said. "Even if it's just one kid we can rescue, it's worth it. One out of five hundred. Are you with me?"

Mikey was silent for a moment, then shrugged. "Let's go. I was bored with living anyway."

They passed through the shimmer. The wraiths flew toward them at Cole's presence and Mikey raised his right index finger and wagged it at them. He stalked forward, always a little faster than Cole, whose depression and anxiety mounted as he stared at Mikey's back.

"You're really against trying to save them?"

"I'm against losing what we've got," Mikey said. "What we could have. I'm also ashamed of myself."

"What?"

Mikey stopped and spun around to face him.

"I don't have what you have, Cole. You say you don't have any extra. That's bullshit. Your extra is courage. Your extra is being unable to turn away. I admire the hell out of it. Part of me wants to sip it through a psychic straw. But I hate it at the same time. The implications of it. The endless boy scout crusader trips that have to come with it. I can't deal, and that's my failure but it's also just my reality."

Cole listened, realizing what he was hearing. He swallowed against the dryness in his throat and nodded.

"If you want, I'll just go on alone. I don't think I need the passport. Fangsy will take care of that."

"I don't want to say goodbye. I want you to come back with me."

Cole shook his head. "It's just like you said."

He started walking. The absence of Mikey's footsteps sent a deep loneliness through him. A hollowness his bones had never known even when he stood before his parents' grave. He reached into his coat pocket and felt the metal, remembering the promise of the show and tell. Smiling, he pivoted to explain it all to Mikey. But Mikey wasn't there. The street was the same stretch of emptiness behind him and ahead. Cole wiped his eyes, bowed his head, and moved forward as the road began its steep decline. He encountered the chalk art and stepped on it. What had Mikey called it? *The Education of the Innocents*? Cole spat on the horrible images and made a point of rubbing out certain squares with the toe of his shoe.

It wasn't long before he encountered the painters. He did not shy away from looking at the canvases. He found he could view them with a detached cynicism that shielded his heart from the images of mutilated, savaged children. No face recognizable, no body intact. The painters were all laboring on parental nightmares and Cole remembered Dimwitter's revelry as he recounted standing in front of the TV in his tuxedo, painting the gallery fire. He began to see every painter as Dimwitter and a coldness shot through him. He went to the nearest easel, tore the canvas free and ripped the heavy, wet paper down the center in front of the painter's skeletal face.

"Call it The Judgment of Cole," he said, throwing the pieces on the ground.

The painter's eyes flashed with the fire of the sacred art. He lashed at Cole with his brush, the tip catching him on the coat sleeve of his right arm. A red streak ran from the wrist to the elbow, and a moment later the fabric separated along that line like a scalpel's incision. The painter swiped again, with Cole just dodging, falling against another painter and knocking over both him and his easel.

Cole got up. The painters were starting to surround him, their paint brushes red and sharp. He heard his name shouted from behind their backs. Mikey was there, right hand at his temple, his expression contorted with pain and effort. One by one, the painters shook and turned away as Mikey whispered, "Back to work, back to work, back to work." A trickle of blood came from his nostrils as he cleared a path. He staggered as he reached Cole, who held him tight even as he moved through the crowd of painters who ignored them again. Mikey went on saying, "Back to work" in a whispered delirium.

They cleared the painters and Cole stopped.

"I couldn't. I tried but I couldn't."

"Couldn't what?" Cole said.

"Leave. Guess I'm in it for the long haul. Or the short haul if Fangsy has his way. Whatever haul it is."

Thank you, Cole thought.

"You're welcome. But you've got to get a handle on your anger. I can feel it boiling over. It's going to fuck you over."

They walked together until they reached the musicians, who invested their talents in funeral hymns, adagios too somber and powerful to memorialize any single death. This was music for the fate of nations, songs for the failing world. Cole imagined processions of children's coffins borne on the shoulders of mourning adults. The music came down at them like a taunt, and as they reached the gravesites platoons of artists arrived to vandalize the coffins with their vision, the gathered adults of New Florence shed their grief and exploded into vigorous applause, with voices declaring, "Now their deaths have meaning!" and "How beautiful! Such colors! Makes it all worthwhile in the end!"

Cole felt Mikey's touch on his arm and heard another warning about anger. The rage was too large to ward off. He saw himself snatching away the violins and guitars and smashing them to bits on the street. The action, the sound of the splintering, the satisfaction of the destruction was all so real Cole couldn't believe he hadn't done it as Mikey hurried him through the throng. Mikey was sweating. He claimed Cole's rage was burning him and begged him for control. His eyes were wet. Cole had never seen Mikey like that. It meant something important to him, more important than anything else. Except there was something else. There were the images on the painters' canvases, the songs of the musicians, the imagined voices of the adults praising artists for making the funerals of children beautiful and therefore worthwhile.

Mikey seized his wrist and stared hard into Cole's eyes. For a moment, Cole found he didn't even recognize him.

"Don't you know what's happening?" Mikey said. "Haven't you guessed?"

If he said anything else, Cole didn't hear him. He swooned on his feet and pushed forward along the steepening descent. There, in the middle of the road, he encountered an old woman hunched over a potter's wheel. There were two small baskets on either side of her feet, each covered with lids. Her lap cradled a medical student's dissection bowl, stainless steel and filled with wet strips of pink, flayed skin piled high like spaghetti. A featureless head like a styrofoam wig stand was mounted to a spindle at the wheel's center, making a steady, lazy rotation. As it spun, the woman took strips of flesh and layered them along the head, working and kneading them into a seamless covering. Just this addition made Cole realize the head and face were not very large, about the size of an adolescent boy's. The woman looked over her shoulder at him and smiled.

"Some artists hate being watched," she said, "but I've always done my best work under scrutiny."

Without breaking her stare or losing her smile, the sculptor reached down and flipped the lid on the basket by her right foot. She fished inside, making a sound like someone stirring meatballs through cold noodles. The first eyeball resembled a large spotted marble half-wrapped in a tattered sausage casing, displayed in her palm like some dead polliwog.

"The Master has gifted me with a leftover," she said, and began working the eyeball into place. As soon as it was nested, the eye darted about in all directions and then shed heavy tears.

This sent the sculptor into fits of ecstasy and laughter. "Poor child. Now you are my *art* forever, and I will call you *Crying Boy*. Soon I will hear you thank me for your fate."

She bent to the left basket and retrieved a pair of lips, two red slugs of flesh that seemed joined at the corners with a bit of fraying ribbon. These she slapped against the flesh with little delicacy, pinching and prodding the lips into a crude oval. She forced her fingers into the flesh to work and shape a cavern for the mouth.

STOLEN PALLOR

When the tongue was in place, a boy's voice began to cry out for his parents. How the sculptor shook with joy.

How Cole shook from feverish rage.

"Cole," Mikey said. "Don't."

Don't what? Cole asked himself, looking at the weeping eye. As his gaze deepened, he found himself sharing the panic, the hopelessness, the utter despair and confusion. Hours earlier this boy was on a field trip to the art museum with his life ahead of him. Reduced and perverted now to a monstrous art project destined to sit on a shelf and rot the wood with tears.

Because of me.

All his prior anger, all the rage his whole life had ever known, didn't equal Cole's bloodlust now. He looked back and saw Mikey holding out his hands and talking, but he could not hear his voice. He saw Mikey and everything around him in the same red the painters used, the same red as Fangsy's eyes and lips. His right hand went into his coat pocket and found the metal. He started to squeeze it, a vestigial act of sanity that had no place here. The metal was no weapon, it was round rather than sharp, yet he brought it out like a prison shank and drove it down on the base of the old woman's neck. Cole felt every part of the act. He wanted no disconnect or disassociation. The metal cut into the sculptor's skin. Her flesh yielded like wet, heavy clay, boneless. But not bloodless. A heavy black liquid bubbled out of the wound and down her back as she shrieked. Cole yanked the metal free and struck again, this time driving down on the back of her head. No skull in evidence. The metal lodged deep in her flesh like a shuriken, and he gritted his teeth and yanked it out, skipping away from a fountain gush of blood. The sculptor fell over and Cole kicked her in the stomach and ribs, in the small of the back and in the head. He wiped the metal clean on her skirt. All the while Mikey stood off to the side with both hands over his mouth, while the one eye went on crying.

"Here," Cole said, holding the metal out to Mikey. "What you wanted to see. What I always wanted to show. My magic amulet. I used to pretend it was my father's police badge, melted by the fire. Found in the aftermath. One of Dad's officers gave it to me at the funeral. I've never been without it. Told myself it was Dad's spirit or something. Like it gave me strength."

He shook his hand with emphasis, imploring Mikey to take it. Mikey started to and then refused.

"But I don't need it anymore. I've got something else."

"You're not giving up your past like this," Mikey said. "You're on the verge of committing suicide, Cole. If I take that from you now, I'm accepting the keepsake of a dead man."

"Then don't accept it!"

Cole threw the metal on the ground and stepped on it. As he did, a flash came from underneath him. He felt himself falling through a hole, plummeting and turning, landing in a new place. Still Midnight Village.

Maybe an unmarked graveyard.

A solitary figure stood a few feet away from him, the blue face turned skyward, the red lips curved in a serene smile. As Cole stood up, the face swung down, and red eyes regarded him with evident pleasure.

"At last."

Cole looked around for any sign of the children. Fangsy seemed to understand his purpose, and he laughed and shook his head. "They are of no concern to you now."

"They're why I came!"

"Oh no," he said. "You came because your long study in the sacred art nears its end. You cannot pretend otherwise. Come. Learn how your journey started."

Fangsy moved across the barren field of their meeting place and Cole followed him to a single freestanding wall. There were no other buildings around. The wall stretched and wound its way into the unseen distance like a half-completed labyrinth.

STOLEN PALLOR

The air carried a strong reek of decay. Gray, withered body parts were strewn along the ground. Fangsy stepped on the pieces as he moved to the start of the wall. He gestured and Cole came closer. The wall, which seemed blank at first, revealed it contained a fresco.

A continuous, magnificent art piece.

Fangsy moved on but he did not summon Cole to follow. Cole stood staring at a depiction of fifteen simple wood-frame homes with thatched roofs, arranged almost in a circle, with a vast forest encroaching on all sides. The thatch seemed to leap out at him, and he touched one to confirm a suspicion. Several locks of dyed hair had been affixed to the roofs to represent straw. He swept his fingertips to the left, feeling the different textures that made up the surrounding trees. Fragments of bone, teeth, dried viscera, tanned skin. Every conceivable part of the anatomy, scraps of brain and slices of spleen, testicles and vulvas, tonsils and nipples, shin bones and eyelashes. A mixed media of paint and body parts, pieced together in painstaking, seamless detail.

Figures stood outside each house, positioned before easels made from delicate bones, little squares of flesh for mounted canvas. Five canvases displayed miniature paintings, and four of the cameos showed breathtaking beauty and detail, as if rendered under a jeweler's loupe. The fifth was crude, a child's stick figure work. It seemed to be front and center, meant to draw the eye. Why spotlight terrible art?

Fangsy had stopped several yards up ahead and stood admiring another part of the fresco. Cole was in no hurry to reach him. He walked along the wall, his attention never off the scrolling image. He now saw a man standing alone in a grove, painting a crude demonic figure on his canvas even as the figure appeared in front of him. A summoning through art, Cole thought, noting the distinct difference between the crude portrait and the details of the real thing. The point seemed clear. *This* Faust was a dauber looking to become Da Vinci.

The deal was struck, the artist on his knees, head tilted back to receive communion. The demon cut its own wrist and bled down the man's throat, the blood so red and thick Cole was sure it must have been actual paint running from the demon's veins. As Cole kept moving, he learned how the pact was sealed. Murders followed, and black souls escaped each body and circled in the sky overhead. Soon only one figure stood outside the clutch of houses, painting self-portrait after self-portrait. The fresco rendered them in full detail, side-by-side. The first showed a young man with windswept auburn hair, a pale face, almost bloodless lips. The third face was an exact duplicate of the self-portrait in the Founders' Room. The faces formed an inexorable evolution towards Fangsy's present guise.

"Come. Your genealogy is long and complicated and should be obvious to you now. I wish to reveal your progeny."

Cole stood still, not understanding the meaning. Fangsy called to him again. He went and the story of New Florence and Midnight Village progressed decades at a time at his right shoulder.

"The original colony stood on this very spot," Fangsy said. "I intended to make it a garden of dark delights. The other city, the *pretender* city, were weeds that grew beyond all control. I watched the buildings grow, casting shade upon my work. I called upon my master and teacher for help, but my pleas were met with laughter. Then I understood the nature of our pact. My creative powers would grow without limit, but it was doomed to the shade. My masterpieces would go unnoticed. I was the inheritor, the reviver, the torch bearer of a sacred art older than any rude sketch primitive man ever made in the dirt."

Fangsy pulled him much further along the fresco. Cole saw the rise of New Florence's skyline, the creation of the Crayon Box. Each skyscraper was rendered in exacting detail, a mosaic of molars dyed and lacquered like pieces of ceramic. Red streaks ran down the buildings like tears.

"I've done great work this day."

"This was done today?"

"All of it," Fangsy said, gesturing down the entire length of the wall.

"That's impossible. This would take years."

"A genius can work very fast if he has the materials on hand."

He stroked one of the buildings. "There are over three hundred teeth in this composition alone. Lean in. Listen. Do you hear the overlapping cries from the twelve children whose mouths were sacrificed?"

Cole stepped back, shaken. Fangsy stared at him like a genius disgusted by a simpleton.

"Is your mind so plodding it can't appreciate the symbolism of the teeth? Each of these buildings nibble and gnaw on my intended legacy. The skyscrapers grow and cast their shadows. But dark roses grow best in cold shade. In this way *my* artist's colony has thrived despite neither public acknowledgement or appreciation. Thanks to you, both are imminent."

The fresco scrolled along faster than Cole could follow as Fangsy dragged him along. They stopped at the depiction of *Gone By Morning*. The rise of the glass walls. The glass ceiling capping it off followed by the black drapes, represented now by Fangsy's shadowy hand descending from the sky. The drapes were a weaving of eyelashes, the glass an execution of fingernails peeled from the living and clarified by hot tears.

So Fangsy explained.

"Here is where my great masterpiece was conceived. A new way of thinking about both my own creativity and the sacred art. I have lived very long and observed how little the world of art has changed. Art is a place where bravado and bluff make adequate currency, and posturing pays the bills. So it was in the beginning, so it was in the ever-since. New Florence attracts cultured men and women whose taste for finer things lags behind their confidence in identifying them. One sniffs it in their flesh, tastes it in their blood—a genuine anxiety and frustration with themselves, a self-doubt about the palate of their life. They are box wine drinkers desperate to be sommeliers, putting on airs because they cannot really discern a rare vintage from the various wine bouquets of existence, the *aroma of chocolate* in their romantic lives, the *robust tannins* flavoring their sage financial investments, the *notes of gushing dark currants* they seek for their souls while moving from one spiritual crisis to another. Yet friends assure them vérité can be found in the correct piece of art. Projected confidence, false or true, burns beacon-bright for such people and draws them to the projector, making them eager to listen, eager to nod, eager to touch, eager to buy.

"So it was for the Directorate when I sent Dimwitter to convince them of the existence of the great, mysterious Fangsy, whose art was about to shake the world. How eager they were to make New Florence the epicenter of the quake. See here how the fire burns? Notice how the flames glisten? I shaved the epithelium from the eyes of thirty fourth graders to achieve the delicate layering effect. Now see—"

"Stop!"

"*Now see* the dark figure in the lower right corner of the bottom pane? You may need to lean close."

Fangsy shoved Cole by the back of his head until his nose mashed flat against the wall. He went cross-eyed before he saw what Fangsy indicated. The black speck he'd pointed out was Cole as a boy, beating on the glass, screaming. Every detail perfect. Cole thrashed, trying to pull back. Fangsy held him in place and leaned in close to his ear.

"Dad, Dad, where are you? Dad, I can't find you."

It was an uncanny imitation of his boyhood voice. Cole shook. The dream exploded across his vision, replacing the fresco, and he wept. He made fists out of his hands and beat at the fresco as best he could, breaking his knuckles on the wall as he cried out, "You bastard! You fucking bastard!"

"Yes, such beautiful hate, a lava flow of it from my beautiful phoenix."

"I'm not your anything!"

"So wrong, so very wrong. Come, look, take the next few steps. See my work completed, so close now, on the precipice of finality."

Fangsy hauled Cole up and flung him along the ground. Cole kicked and crawled ahead of his pursuer, no strategic thought in his head. He was just reacting now. Glimpses of fresco still caught his eye. Was that him and Mikey in the bedroom, holding each other? Why would that be there? Cole couldn't focus on the question. There was something greater to catch his eyes, something more certain. A handful of children standing in a cluster, stripped down, looking lobotomized. Cole crawled to them, trying to wrap his arms around them. So few. So very few.

He was sobbing.

"Let them go. You've got me now. Don't hurt them."

"I never waste supplies," Fangsy said.

Cole clenched his jaw.

Fangsy took a girl and a boy and led them to the edge of the fresco. He touched their faces with the edge of his paintbrush. Cole tensed, holding his breath, afraid any movement would bring harm to the children. He made a whimpering plea for mercy.

"That's just what they get. The others joined the fresco piecemeal."

Fangsy swiped his brush against the wall, leaving a glowing tear in the brick. He pushed the girl against it and she was decanted through, reappearing on the other side, a painted rendition of herself, frozen in an expression of loss and fear. The boy joined her a moment later, their haunted expressions locked, eternalized. Cole dropped his gaze to his feet in loss.

"Had you accepted yesterday's invitation, you would

have seen the true *Gone By Morning*. Your father's face looks very much like theirs. Put your ear near their mouths and you will hear their cries. No? You won't listen? Does your blood boil to save them?"

"Yes," Cole said, his voice so husky he had trouble saying the word.

"Will you not strike me? Stop me? If your blood is as you claim. Perhaps the children's lives don't mean as much as you say."

Fangsy took another boy and led him to the wall.

"These are the children of true vampires, the fake and phony artists of New Florence whose garish colors would steal the glory of my pallor. I hate them and their seed. I enjoy every moment of their torment. My art grows from it. I feel my masterpiece gathering strength. On the pulse of its existence. On the tip of glory's tongue."

He shoved the boy through the cut and added him to the fresco. Cole lunged at Fangsy, provoking a backhand that crumpled him at the monster's feet. He rolled onto his back as Fangsy said, "A heartbeat starting. But the children are not enough. My masterpiece needs more fuel and I know the one thing that will suffice."

Fangsy's brush made another slashing motion, leaving a glowing slit in the air. He reached through, arm disappearing a few seconds before he jerked it back with Mikey in his clutches.

"No!" Cole shouted, pushing himself up. Fangsy held Mikey high in the air by his throat. His legs kicked, his bulging eyes shifting over to Cole. He made a pathetic noise, maybe an attempt to say Cole's name. Cole went to his knees like any desperate supplicant and begged for Mikey's life. Fangsy cursed him for obtuseness, looked at Mikey's dying eyes and said, "Masterpiece, masterpiece."

Cole made another plea and was kicked aside. He offered himself again and again, trading his life for the kids, for Mikey, for all of them. He asked Fangsy to imprison him in the fresco. What did Fangsy want? What would he accept?

He just kept saying, "Masterpiece."

Cole screamed at the starless sky until he heard the smallest sound, *clink*, to his right. Mikey had either dropped or thrown his father's melted badge and Cole held it against his chest like a rosary and gripped for all his worth. His body spasmed. His tears were hotter than anything he'd ever experienced. They carried the heat of the fire that killed his father, the heat of his desire to make Fangsy desolate and ruined, to humiliate him before delivering the killing blow. His anger toward the potter had been immediate, reactionary. Seeing Mikey's life draining away, his imagination flourished with a premeditation and creativity that obliterated every boundary of sanity or morality he possessed.

Sometimes evil just wins.

Mikey managed the faintest moan. Cole winced, not from the sound but because his hands were cut on the metal and bleeding. His vision, fixed on the starless, Godless sky, dipped to follow the length of the fresco. He gazed into the past, desperation drawn to desperation. He saw the summoned entity. Nameless. Proven only by Fangsy himself. Proof enough. As for names, when it came to soul dealing, perhaps only the thought need count.

With blood dripping off the metal, Cole launched his prayer, broad enough to be cast onto the open waters of dark faith, where maybe all gods belonged to a single body of hate. He prayed in his father's name and Mikey's. He prayed for the face of every stolen, broken child. He spat his prayer and kept spitting it.

The metal warmed in his hand. It was changing, getting longer, sharper. Fresh and malleable from the forge inside him. His inner artisan hammered away at its new shape. A bright red glow enveloped it, redder than Fangsy's eyes and lips. The light broke across his face and lifted him. He was on his feet and strong, powerful, vengeful.

His father's voice spoke in his head.

What can I offer, son?

Cole looked at Fangsy and then at the metal, now a vicious dagger in his right hand. He grinned.

Fangsy froze and let Mikey fall. "Teacher?" he said. His tone almost innocent. "Teacher, do you approve my achievement?" Cole answered with the lesson and he taught it with the dagger. Taught it over and over. Taught it on Fangsy's face and neck, torso, arms, and legs. Fangsy answered in the rote screams Cole wanted to hear. He became a blue and black lump on the ground and Cole went on lecturing. He rolled Fangsy onto his back and prepared to drive the dagger between his red eyes. Before he could, Fangsy's dying breaths carried a fading laugh from a mouth curved up in a triumphant smile. His right hand caressed through Cole's hair, a first and final stroke.

"Your rage, your sorrow, your whole life since. It is you—you alone. Always you. My one true masterpiece, my long and patient work, my tribute to the sacred art. Completed at last. Masterpiece, masterpiece. Not a painting but a sculpture. A monument to stand next to *David*. I call it—*Cole*."

ABOUT THE AUTHORS

Sean Eads is a writer and librarian from Denver, Colorado. He is the author of 5 novels and 1 short story collection, and has been a finalist for the Lambda Literary Award, the Shirley Jackson Award, and the Colorado Book Award. His next novel, *Lost Story,* is about Ernest Hemingway. You can find him online at www.seaneads.net.

Joshua Viola is a Colorado Book Award winner and Splatterpunk Award nominee. He edited the *Denver Post* #1 bestselling horror anthology, *Nightmares Unhinged,* and co-edited *Cyber World*—named one of the best science fiction anthologies of 2016 by Barnes & Noble. He is the co-author of the comic book slasher series *True Believers* with Stephen Graham Jones, which features official cameos by Jamie Lee Curtis, R.L. Stine, Matt Heafy, GWAR, Devon Sawa, Jeffrey Combs, and more. As a producer, he has worked on films like Skinner's *Shrine of Abominations, Deathgasm 2: Goremageddon,* and most recently with Slash of Guns N' Roses on Steven Kostanski's *Deathstalker* reboot. As a videogame developer, he worked on *Pirates of the Caribbean: Call of the Kraken* and *TARGET: Terror.* He is co-owner of Bit Bot Media with Hollywood musician, Klayton (Celldweller), co-owner of Metal X Entertainment with Bram Stoker Award winner James Aquilone, and the owner and chief editor of Hex Publishers. He lives in Denver, Colorado, with his husband and son. Learn more at JoshuaViola.com

Join Blood Bound Books
Newsletter for updates and to
receive 20% off your next order at
www.BloodBoundBooks.com

www.ingramcontent.com/pod-product-compliance
Lightning Source LLC
Chambersburg PA
CBHW052012170626
46808CB00007B/2899